W9-ADM-514

A
Gift
of
DRAGONS

A Del Rey® Book
Published by The Ballantine Publishing Group

www.delreydigital.com

Library of Congress Cataloging-in-Publication Data is available
upon request.

ISBN 0-345-45635-1

Book design by C. Linda Dingler

Manufactured in the United States of America

First Edition: November 2002

10 9 8 7 6 5 4 3 2 1

ANNE McCAFFREY

A Gift
of
DRAGONS

Ballantine Books
New York

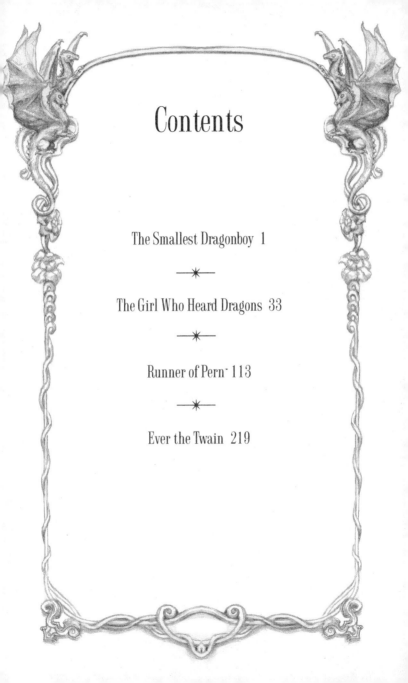

Contents

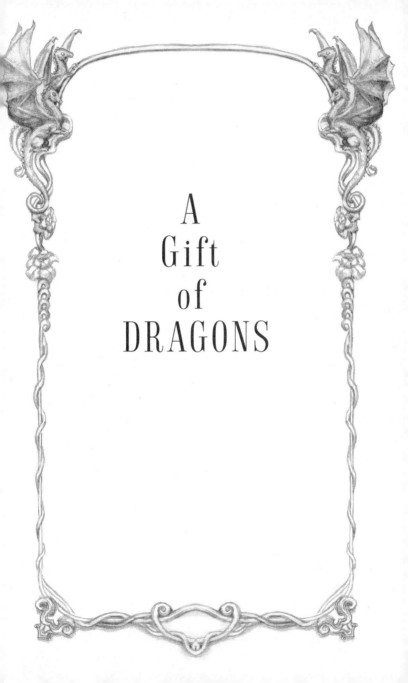

A
Gift
of
DRAGONS

THE
SMALLEST
DRAGONBOY

*A*lthough Keevan lengthened his walking stride as far as his legs would stretch, he couldn't quite keep up with the other candidates. He knew he would be teased again.

Just as he knew many other things that his foster mother told him he ought not to know, Keevan knew that Beterli, the most senior of the boys, set that spanking pace just to embarrass him, the smallest dragonboy. Keevan would arrive, tail fork-end of the group, breathless, chest heaving, and maybe get a stern look from the instructing wingsecond.

Dragonriders, even if they were still only hopeful candidates for the glowing eggs which were hardening on the hot sands of the Hatching Ground cavern, were expected to be punctual and prepared. Sloth was not tolerated by the Weyrleader of Benden Weyr. A good record was especially important now. It was very near hatching time, when the baby dragons would crack their mottled shells, and stagger forth to choose their lifetime companions. The very thought of that glorious moment made

Keevan's breath catch in his throat. To be chosen—
to be a dragonrider! To sit astride the neck of a
winged beast with jeweled eyes: to be his friend, in
telepathic communion with him for life; to be his
companion in good times and fighting extremes; to
fly effortlessly over the lands of Pern! Or, thrillingly,
between to any point anywhere on the world! Flying
between was done on dragonback or not at all, and it
was dangerous.

Keevan glanced upward, past the black mouths of
the weyr caves in which grown dragons and their
chosen riders lived, toward the Star Stones that
crowned the ridge of the old volcano that was
Benden Weyr. On the height, the blue watch dragon,
his rider mounted on his neck, stretched the great
transparent pinions that carried him on the winds
of Pern to fight the evil Thread that fell at certain
times from the skies. The many-faceted rainbow
jewels of his eyes glistened fleetingly in the greeny
sun. He folded his great wings to his back, and the
watch pair resumed their statuelike pose of alert-
ness.

Then the enticing view was obscured as Keevan
passed into the Hatching Ground cavern. The sands
underfoot were hot, even through heavy wher-hide
boots. How the bootmaker had protested having to

sew so small! Keevan was forced to wonder why being small was reprehensible. People were always calling him "babe" and shooing him away as being "too small" or "too young" for this or that. Keevan was constantly working, twice as hard as any other boy his age, to prove himself capable. What if his muscles weren't as big as Beterli's? They were just as hard. And if he couldn't overpower anyone in a wrestling match, he could outdistance everyone in a footrace.

"Maybe if you run fast enough," Beterli had jeered on the occasion when Keevan had been goaded to boast of his swiftness, "you could catch a dragon. That's the only way you'll make a dragonrider!"

"You just wait and see, Beterli, you just wait," Keevan had replied. He would have liked to wipe the contemptuous smile from Beterli's face, but the guy didn't fight fair even when a wingsecond was watching. "No one knows what Impresses a dragon!"

"They've got to be able to *find* you first, babe!"

Yes, being the smallest candidate was not an enviable position. It was therefore imperative that Keevan Impress a dragon in his first hatching. That would wipe the smile off every face in the cavern, and accord him the respect due any dragonrider, even the smallest one.

Besides, no one knew exactly what Impressed the baby dragons as they struggled from their shells in search of their lifetime partners.

"I like to believe that dragons see into a man's heart," Keevan's foster mother, Mende, told him. "If they find goodness, honesty, a flexible mind, patience, courage—and you've got that in quantity, dear Keevan—that's what dragons look for. I've seen many a well-grown lad left standing on the sands, Hatching Day, in favor of someone not so strong or tall or handsome. And if my memory serves me"—which it usually did: Mende knew every word of every Harper's tale worth telling, although Keevan did not interrupt her to say so—"I don't believe that F'lar, our Weyrleader, was all that tall when bronze Mnementh chose him. And Mnementh was the only bronze dragon of that hatching."

Dreams of Impressing a bronze were beyond Keevan's boldest reflections, although that goal dominated the thoughts of every

KEEVAN

other hopeful candidate. Green dragons were small and fast and more numerous. There was more prestige to Impressing a blue or brown than a green. Being practical, Keevan seldom dreamed as high as a big fighting brown, like Canth, F'nor's fine fellow, the biggest brown on all Pern. But to fly a bronze? Bronzes were almost as big as the queen, and only they took the air when a queen flew at mating time. A bronze rider could aspire to become Weyrleader! Well, Keevan would console himself, brown riders could aspire to become wingseconds, and that wasn't bad. He'd even settle for a green dragon: they were small, but so was he. No matter! He simply had to Impress a dragon his first time in the Hatching Ground. Then no one in the Weyr would taunt him anymore for being so small.

Shells, Keevan thought now, but the sands are hot!

"Impression time is imminent, candidates," the wingsecond was saying as everyone crowded respectfully close to him. "See the extent of the striations on this promising egg." The stretch marks *were* larger than yesterday.

Everyone leaned forward and nodded thoughtfully. That particular egg was the one Beterli had marked as his own, and no other candidate dared, on pain of being beaten by Beterli at his first opportunity, to approach it. The egg was marked by a large yellowish splotch in the shape of a dragon backwinging to land, talons outstretched to grasp rock. Everyone knew that bronze eggs bore distinctive markings. And naturally, Beterli, who'd been presented at eight Impressions already and was the biggest of the candidates, had chosen it.

"I'd say that the great opening day is almost upon us," the wingsecond went on, and then his face assumed a grave expression. "As we well know, there are only forty eggs and seventy-two candidates. Some of you may be disappointed on the great day. That doesn't necessarily mean you aren't dragonrider material, just that *the* dragon for you hasn't been shelled. You'll have other hatchings, and it's no disgrace to be left behind an Impression or two. Or more."

Keevan was positive that the wingsecond's eyes rested on Beterli, who'd been stood off at so many Impressions already. Keevan tried to squinch down so the wingsecond wouldn't notice him. Keevan had been reminded too often that he was eligible to be a candidate by one day only. He, of all the hopefuls, was most likely to be left standing on the great day. One more reason why he simply had to Impress at his first hatching.

"Now move about among the eggs," the wingsecond said. "Touch them. We don't know that it does any good, but it certainly doesn't do any harm."

Some of the boys laughed nervously, but everyone immediately began to circulate among the eggs. Beterli stepped up officiously to "his" egg, daring anyone to come near it. Keevan smiled, because he had already touched it—every inspection day, when the others were leaving the Hatching Ground and no one could see him crouch to stroke it.

Keevan had an egg he concentrated on, too, one drawn slightly to the far side of the others. The shell had a soft greenish-blue tinge with a faint creamy swirl design. The consensus was that this egg contained a mere green, so Keevan was rarely bothered by rivals. He was somewhat perturbed then to see Beterli wandering over to him.

"I don't know why you're allowed in this Impression Keevan. There are enough of us without a babe," Beterli said, shaking his head.

"I'm of age." Keevan kept his voice level, telling himself not to be bothered by mere words.

"Yah!" Beterli made a show of standing on his toe tips. "You can't even see over an egg; Hatching Day, you better get in front or the dragons won't see you at all. 'Course, you could get run down that way in the mad scramble. Oh, I forget, you can run fast, can't you?"

"You'd better make sure a dragon sees *you*, this time, Beterli," Keevan replied. "You're almost over-age, aren't you?"

Beterli flushed and took a step forward, hand halfraised. Keevan stood his ground, but if Beterli advanced one more step, he would call the wingsecond. No one fought on the Hatching Ground. Surely Beterli knew that much.

Fortunately, at that moment, the wingsecond called the boys together and led them from the Hatching Ground to start on evening chores. There were "glows" to be replenished in the main kitchen caverns and sleeping cubicles, the major hallways, and the queen's apartment. Firestone sacks had to be filled against Thread attack, and black rock brought to the kitchen hearths. The boys fell to their chores, tantalized by the odors of roasting meat. The population of the Weyr began to assemble for the evening meal, and the dragonriders came in from the Feeding Ground on their sweep checks.

It was the time of day Keevan liked best: once the chores were done but before dinner was served, a fellow could often get close enough to the dragonriders to hear their talk. Tonight, Keevan's father, K'last,

was at the main dragonrider table. It puzzled Keevan how his father, a brown rider and a tall man, could *be* his father—because he, Keevan, was so small. It obviously puzzled K'last, too, when he deigned to notice his small son: "In a few more Turns, you'll be as tall as I am—or taller!"

K'last was pouring Benden wine all around the table. The dragonriders were relaxing. There'd be no Thread attack for three more days, and they'd be in the mood to tell tall tales, better than Harper yarns, about impossible maneuvers they'd done a-dragonback. When Thread attack was closer, their talk would change to a discussion of tactics of evasion, of going *between*, how long to suspend there until the burning but fragile Thread would freeze and crack and fall harmlessly off dragon and man. They would dispute the exact moment to feed firestone to the dragon so he'd have the best flame ready to sear Thread midair and render it harmless to ground—and man—below. There was such a lot to know and understand about being a dragonrider that sometimes Keevan was overwhelmed. How would he ever be able to remember everything he ought to know at the right moment? He couldn't dare ask such a question; this would only have given additional weight to the notion that he was too young yet to be a dragonrider.

"Having older candidates makes good sense," L'vel was saying, as Keevan settled down near the table. "Why waste four to five years of a dragon's fighting prime until his rider grows up enough to stand the rigors?" L'vel had Impressed a blue of Ramoth's first clutch. Most of the candidates thought L'vel was marvelous because he spoke up in front of the older riders, who awed them. "That was well enough in the Interval when you didn't need to mount the full Weyr complement to fight Thread. But not now. Not with more eligible candidates than ever. Let the babes wait."

"Any boy who is over twelve Turns has the right to stand in the Hatching Ground," K'last replied, a slight smile on his face. He never argued or got angry. Keevan wished he were more like his father. And oh, how he wished he were a brown rider! "Only a dragon—each particular dragon—knows what he wants in a rider. We certainly can't tell. Time and again the theorists," K'last's smile deepened as his eyes swept those at the table, "are surprised by dragon choice. *They* never seem to make mistakes, however."

"Now, K'last, just look at the roster this Impression. Seventy-two boys and only forty eggs. Drop off the twelve youngest, and there's still a good field for the hatchlings to choose from. Shells! There are a couple of weyrlings unable to see over a wher egg much less a dragon! And years before they can ride Thread."

"True enough, but the Weyr is scarcely under fighting strength, and if the youngest Impress, they'll be old enough to fight when the oldest of our current dragons go *between* from senility."

"Half the Weyr-bred lads have already been through several Impressions," one of the bronze riders said then. "I'd say drop some of *them* off this time. Give the untried a chance."

"There's nothing wrong in presenting a clutch with as wide a choice as possible," said the Weyrleader, who had joined the table with Lessa, the Weyrwoman.

"Has there ever been a case," she said, smiling in her odd way at the riders, "where a hatchling didn't choose?"

Her suggestion was almost heretical and drew astonished gasps from everyone, including the boys.

F'lar laughed. "You say the most outrageous things, Lessa."

"Well, *has* there ever been a case where a dragon didn't choose?"

"Can't say as I recall one," K'last replied.

"Then we continue in this tradition," Lessa said firmly, as if that ended the matter.

But it didn't. The argument ranged from one table to the other all through dinner, with some favoring a weeding out of the candidates to the most likely, lopping off those who were very young or who had had multiple opportunities to Impress. All the candidates were in a swivet, though such a departure from tradition would be to the advantage of many. As the evening progressed, more riders were favoring eliminating the youngest and those who'd passed four or more Impressions unchosen. Keevan felt he could bear such a dictum only if Beterli were also eliminated. But this seemed less likely than that Keevan would be turfed out, since the Weyr's need was for fighting dragons and riders.

By the time the evening meal was over, no decision had been reached, although the Weyrleader had promised to give the matter due consideration.

He might have slept on the problem, but few of the candidates did. Tempers were uncertain in the sleeping caverns next morning as the boys were routed out of their beds to carry water and black rock and cover the "glows." Twice Mende had to call Keevan to order for clumsiness.

"Whatever is the matter with you, boy?" she demanded in exasperation when he tipped black rock short of the bin and sooted up the hearth.

"They're going to keep me from this Impression."

"What?" Mende stared at him. "Who?"

"You heard them talking at dinner last night. They're going to turf the babes from the hatching."

Mende regarded him a moment longer before touching his arm gently. "There's lots of talk around a supper table, Keevan. And it cools as soon as the supper. I've heard the same nonsense before every hatching, but nothing is ever changed."

"There's always a first time," Keevan answered, copying one of her own phrases.

"That'll be enough of that, Keevan. Finish your job. If the clutch does hatch today, we'll need full rock bins for the feast, and you won't be around to do the filling. All my fosterlings make dragonriders."

"The first time?" Keevan was bold enough to ask as he scooted off with the rockbarrow.

Perhaps, Keevan thought later, if he hadn't been on that chore just when Beterli was also fetching black rock, things might have turned out differently. But he had dutifully trundled the barrow to the outdoor bunker for another load just as Beterli arrived on a similar errand.

"Heard the news, babe?" Beterli asked. He was grinning from ear to ear, and he put an unnecessary emphasis on the final insulting word.

"The eggs are cracking?" Keevan all but dropped the loaded shovel. Several anxieties flicked through his mind then: he was black with rock dust—would he have time to wash before donning the white tunic of candidacy? And if the eggs were hatching, why hadn't the candidates been recalled by the wingsecond?

"Naw! Guess again!" Beterli was much too pleased with himself.

With a sinking heart, Keevan knew what the news must be, and he could only stare with intense desolation at the older boy.

"C'mon! Guess, babe!"

"I've no time for guessing games," Keevan managed to say with indifference. He began to shovel black rock into the barrow as fast as he could.

"I said, guess." Beterli grabbed the shovel.

"And I said I have no time for guessing games."

Beterli wrenched the shovel from Keevan's hands. "Guess!"

"I'll have that shovel back, Beterli." Keevan straightened up, but he didn't come to Beterli's bulky shoulder. From somewhere, other boys appeared, some with barrows, some mysteriously alerted to the prospect of a confrontation among their numbers.

"Babes don't give orders to candidates around here, babe!"

Someone sniggered and Keevan, incredulous, knew that he must've been dropped from the candidacy.

He yanked the shovel from Beterli's loosened grasp. Snarling, the older boy tried to regain possession, but Keevan clung with all his strength to the handle, dragged back and forth as the stronger boy jerked the shovel about.

With a sudden, unexpected movement, Beterli rammed the handle into Keevan's chest, knocking him over the barrow handles. Keevan felt a sharp, painful jab behind his left ear, an unbearable pain in his left shin, and then a painless nothingness.

Mende's angry voice roused him and, startled, he tried to throw back the covers, thinking he'd overslept. But he couldn't move, so firmly was he tucked into his bed. And then the constriction of a bandage on his head and the dull sickishness in his leg brought back recent occurrences.

"Hatching?" he cried.

"No, lovey," Mende said in a kind voice. Her hand was cool and gentle on his forehead. "Though there's some as won't be at any hatching again." Her voice took on a stern edge.

Keevan looked beyond her to see the Weyrwoman, who was frowning with irritation.

"Keevan, will you tell me what occurred at the black rock bunker?" asked Lessa in an even voice.

He remembered Beterli now and the quarrel over the shovel and . . . what had Mende said about some not being at any hatching? Much as he hated Beterli, he couldn't bring himself to tattle on Beterli and force him out of candidacy.

"Come, lad," and a note of impatience crept into the Weyrwoman's voice. "I merely want to know what happened from you, too. Mende said she sent you for black rock. Beterli—and every Weyrling in the cavern—seems to have been on the same errand. What happened?"

"Beterli took my shovel. I hadn't finished with it."

"There's more than one shovel. What did he *say* to you?"

"He'd heard the news."

"What news?" The Weyrwoman was suddenly amused.

"That . . . that . . . there'd been changes."

"Is that what he said?"

"Not exactly"

"What did he say? C'mon, lad, I've heard from everyone else, you know."

"He said for me to guess the news."

"And you fell for that old gag?" The Weyr-woman's irritation returned.

"Consider all the talk last night at supper, Lessa," Mende said. "Of course the boy would think he'd been eliminated."

"In effect, he is, with a broken skull and leg." Lessa touched his arm in a rare gesture of sympathy. "Be that as it may, Keevan, you'll have other Impressions. Beterli will not. There are certain rules that must be observed by all candidates, and his conduct proves him unacceptable to the Weyr."

She smiled at Mende and then left.

"I'm still a candidate?" Keevan asked urgently.

"Well, you are and you aren't, lovey," his foster mother said. "Is the numbweed working?" she asked, and when he nodded, she said, "You just rest. I'll bring you some nice broth."

At any other time in his life, Keevan would have relished such cosseting, but now he just lay there worrying. Beterli had been dismissed. Would the others think it was his fault? But everyone was there! Beterli provoked that fight. His worry increased, because although he heard excited comings and goings in the passageway, no one tweaked back the curtain across the sleeping alcove he shared with five other boys. Surely one of them would have to come in sometime. No, they were all avoiding him. And something else was wrong. Only he didn't know what.

Mende returned with broth and beachberry bread.

"Why doesn't anyone come see me, Mende? I haven't done anything wrong, have I? I didn't ask to have Beterli turfed out."

Mende soothed him, saying everyone was busy with noontime chores and no one was angry with him. They were giving him a chance to rest in quiet. The numbweed made him drowsy, and her words were fair enough. He permitted his fears to dissipate. Until he heard a hum. Actually, he felt it first, in the broken shinbone and his sore head. The hum began to grow. Two things registered suddenly in

Keevan's groggy mind: the only white candidate's robe still on the pegs in the chamber was his; and the dragons hummed when a clutch was being laid or being hatched. Impression! And he was flat abed.

Bitter, bitter disappointment turned the warm broth sour in his belly. Even the small voice telling him that he'd have other opportunities failed to alleviate his crushing depression. *This* was the Impression that mattered! This was his chance to show *everyone*, from Mende to K'last to L'vel and even the Weyrleader that he, Keevan, was worthy of being a dragonrider.

He twisted in bed, fighting against the tears that threatened to choke him. Dragonmen don't cry! Dragonmen learn to live with pain.

Pain? The leg didn't actually pain him as he rolled about on his bedding. His head felt sort of stiff from the tightness of the bandage. He sat up, an effort in itself since the numbweed made exertion difficult. He touched the splinted leg; the knee was unhampered. He had no feeling in his bone, really. He swung himself carefully to the side of his bed and stood slowly. The room wanted to swim about him. He closed his eyes, which made the dizziness worse, and he had to clutch the wall.

Gingerly, he took a step. The broken leg dragged.

It hurt in spite of the numbweed, but what was pain to a dragonman?

No one had said he couldn't go to the Impression. "You are and you aren't," were Mende's exact words.

Clinging to the wall, he jerked off his bedshirt. Stretching his arm to the utmost, he jerked his white candidate's tunic from the peg. Jamming first one arm and then the other into the holes, he pulled it over his head. Too bad about the belt. He couldn't wait. He hobbled to the door, hung on to the curtain to steady himself. The weight on his leg was unwieldy. He wouldn't get very far without something to lean on. Down by the bathing pool was one of the long crook-necked poles used to retrieve clothes from the hot washing troughs. But it was down there, and he was on the level above. And there was no one nearby to come to his aid: everyone would be in the Hatching Ground right now, eagerly waiting for the first egg to crack.

The humming increased in volume and tempo, an urgency to which Keevan responded, knowing that his time was all too limited if he was to join the ranks of the hopeful boys standing around the cracking eggs. But if he hurried down the ramp, he'd fall flat on his face.

He could, of course, go flat on his rear end, the way crawling children did. He sat down, sending a jarring stab of pain through his leg and up to the wound on the back of his head. Gritting his teeth and blinking away tears, Keevan scrabbled down the ramp. He had to wait a moment at the bottom to catch his breath. He got to one knee, the injured leg straight out in front of him. Somehow, he managed to push himself erect, though the room seemed about to tip over his ears. It wasn't far to the crooked stick, but it seemed an age before he had it in his hand.

Then the humming stopped!

Keevan cried out and began to hobble frantically across the cavern, out to the bowl of the Weyr. Never had the distance between living caverns and the Hatching Ground seemed so great. Never had the Weyr been so breathlessly silent. It was as if the multitude of people and dragons watching the hatching held every breath in suspense. Not even the wind muttered down the steep sides of the bowl. The only sounds to break the stillness were Keevan's ragged gasps and the thump-thud of his stick on the hardpacked ground. Sometimes he had to hop twice on his good leg to maintain his balance. Twice he fell into the sand and had to pull himself up on the stick,

his white tunic no longer spotless. Once he jarred himself so badly he couldn't get up immediately.

Then he heard the first exhalation of the crowd, the oohs, the muted cheer, the susurrus of excited whispers. *An egg had cracked*, and the dragon had chosen his rider. Desperation increased Keevan's hobble. Would he never reach the arching mouth of the Hatching Ground?

Another cheer and an excited spate of applause spurred Keevan to greater effort. If he didn't get there in moments, there'd be no unpaired hatchling left. Then he was actually staggering into the Hatching Ground, the sands hot on his bare feet.

No one noticed his entrance or his halting progress. And Keevan could see nothing but the backs of the white-robed candidates, seventy of them ringing the area around the eggs. Then one side would surge forward or back and there'd be a cheer. Another dragon had been Impressed. Suddenly a large gap appeared in the white human wall, and Keevan had his first sight of the eggs. There didn't seem to be *any* left uncracked, and he could see the lucky boys standing beside wobble-legged dragons. He could hear the unmistakable plaintive crooning of hatchlings and their squawks of protest as they'd fall awkwardly in the sand.

Suddenly he wished that he hadn't left his bed, that he'd stayed away from the Hatching Ground. Now everyone would see his ignominious failure. So he scrambled as desperately to reach the shadowy walls of the Hatching Ground as he had struggled to cross the bowl. He mustn't be seen.

He didn't notice, therefore, that the shifting group of boys remaining had begun to drift in his direction. The hard pace he had set himself and his cruel disappointment took their double toll of Keevan. He tripped and collapsed sobbing to the warm sands. He didn't see the consternation in the watching Weyrfolk above the Hatching Ground, nor did he hear the excited whispers of speculation. He didn't know that the Weyrleader and Weyrwoman had dropped to the arena and were making their way toward the knot of boys slowly moving in the direction of the entrance.

"Never seen anything like it," the Weyrleader was saying. "Only thirty-nine riders chosen. And the bronze trying to leave the Hatching Ground without making Impression."

"A case in point of what I said last night," the Weyrwoman replied, "where a hatchling makes no choice because the right boy isn't there."

"There's only Beterli and K'last's young one missing. And there's a full wing of likely boys to choose from . . ."

"None acceptable, apparently. Where is the creature going? He's not heading for the entrance after all. Oh, what have we there, in the shadows?"

Keevan heard with dismay the sound of voices nearing him. He tried to burrow into the sand. The mere thought of how he would be teased and taunted now was unbearable.

Don't worry! Please don't worry! The thought was urgent, but not his own.

Someone kicked sand over Keevan and butted roughly against him.

"Go away. Leave me alone!" he cried.

Why? was the injured-sounding question inserted into his mind. There was no voice, no tone, but the question was there, perfectly clear, in his head.

Incredulous, Keevan lifted his head and stared into the glowing jeweled eyes of a small bronze dragon. His wings were wet, the tips drooping in the sand. And he sagged in the middle on his unsteady

legs, although he was making a great effort to keep erect.

Keevan dragged himself to his knees, oblivious of the pain in his leg. He wasn't even aware that he was ringed by the boys passed over, while thirty-one pairs of resentful eyes watched him Impress the dragon. The Weyrmen looked on, amused, and surprised at the draconic choice, which could not be forced. Could not be questioned. Could not be changed.

Why? asked the dragon again. *Don't you like me?* His eyes whirled with anxiety, and his tone was so piteous that Keevan staggered forward and threw his arms around the dragon's neck, stroking his eye ridges, patting the damp, soft hide, opening the fragile-looking wings to dry them, and wordlessly assuring the hatchling over and over again that he was the most perfect, most beautiful, most beloved dragon in the Weyr, in all the Weyrs of Pern.

"What's his name, K'van?" asked Lessa, smiling warmly at the new dragonrider. K'van stared up at her for a long moment. Lessa would know as soon as he did. Lessa was the only person who could "receive" from all dragons, not only her own Ramoth. Then he gave her a radiant smile, recognizing the traditional shortening of his name that raised him forever to the rank of dragonrider.

My name is Heth, the dragon thought mildly, then hiccuped in sudden urgency. *I'm hungry*.

"Dragons are born hungry," said Lessa, laughing. "F'lar, give the boy a hand. He can barely manage his own legs, much less a dragon's."

K'van remembered his stick and drew himself up. "We'll be just fine, thank you."

"You may be the smallest dragonrider ever, young K'van," F'lar said, "but you're one of the bravest!"

And Heth agreed! Pride and joy so leaped in both chests that K'van wondered if his heart would burst right out of his body. He looped an arm around Heth's neck and the pair, the smallest dragonboy and the hatchling who wouldn't choose anybody else, walked out of the Hatching Ground together forever.

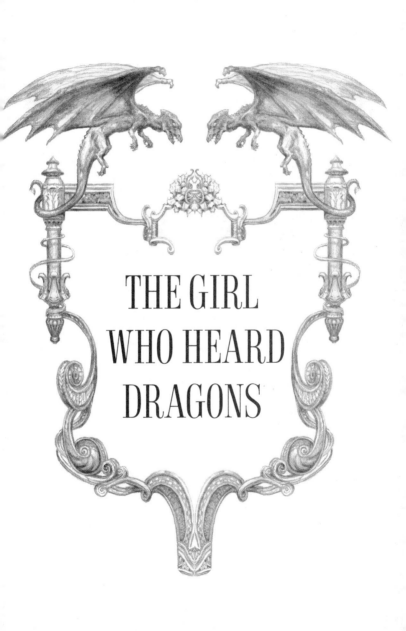

THE GIRL
WHO HEARD
DRAGONS

*A*ramina was roused by the urgency of her parents' voices. Dowell's fierce whisper of persuasion and her mother's a fearful rejoinder. She lay still, at first thinking that her mother had had another of her "seeings," but on such occasions Barla's voice was totally devoid of emotion. Straining her ears to pick up only her parents' words, Aramina ignored the myriad nocturnal noises of the enormous Igen cavern that sheltered some of the hundreds of holdless folk on Pern.

"It is pointless to assign blame at this juncture, Barla," her father was whispering, "or to moan about our pride in Aramina's ability. We must leave. Now. Tonight."

"But winter comes," Barla wailed. "How will we survive?"

"I can't say that we survived all that well here last winter, with so many to share out what game was caught," Dowell said as he rapidly stuffed oddments into the capacious pack. "I've heard tell of caves in Lemos. And Lemos . . ."

"Has wood!" There was bitterness in Barla's voice. "And none in Igen to suit you."

"We may be holdless, woman, but we have not lost honor and dignity. I will not be party to Lady Holdless Thella's designs. I will not permit our daughter to be exploited in such a way. Gather your things. Now. I'll wake the children."

When Dowell touched Aramina's shoulder, she swallowed against her fear. She hadn't liked the self-styled Lady Holdless Thella when Thella had sought her out on the last few visits to the Igen caverns to recruit people to her roving bands. Aramina had been fascinated, and obliquely repelled by Giron, Thella's second-in-command, the dragonless man who had scrutinized her so intently that Aramina had been hard put not to squirm under his cold and empty eyes. A man who had been a dragonrider and lost his dragon was only half a man, or so everyone said. Thella had hinted at concessions for Aramina's family, perhaps even a hold, though Aramina was not so stupid as to contest that possibility, even as Thella offered the bait. Nor did Thella's argument that the holdless had to band together, sharing whatever possessions they had, hold any weight with a child who had early learned that no gift was free.

"I'm sorry, Father," she murmured in fearful contrition.

"Sorry? For what, child? Oh, you heard? You are not at fault, 'Mina. Can you manage your sister? We must leave now."

Aramina nodded. She rose and deftly twisted her blanket about her shoulders to make a sling for Nexa. She had carried her thus often as the small family had wandered eastward. Indeed, Nexa merely draped herself sleepily across Aramina's bony young shoulder and snuggled into the supporting blanket without rousing from her deep slumber.

Aramina glanced about, unconsciously checking to see that every one of their few belongings had been reclaimed.

"I've already packed the wagon with what we could take," Dowell said.

"And Mother thought that that thieving Nerat family was pilfering things again." Aramina was somewhat exasperated because she had been obliged to spend an entire day surreptitiously near that noisome camp, trying to spot any of their belongings.

Barla had already gathered up her precious cooking pots, wrapping them in old clothes to prevent their banging. Another shawl held the rest of the family's portables, zealously guarded against the pilfering habits of the cavern's population.

"Hush now! Come. We must make the most of the full moons."

For the first time Aramina regretted that her father's skill with woods had purchased for his family a partially secluded alcove toward the rear of the great Igen cavern. It had been much cooler during the blazing Igen summer, warmer and sheltered from the bitter winter winds, but now it seemed an interminable distance as they wended a cautious path among sleeping bodies to reach the entrance of the wind-sculpted sandstone cave.

Frequently Aramina had to shift Nexa in the journey down the sands to the river, sinking occasionally into old refuse holes and trying not to trip over debris. Having no hold to be proud of, the holdless residing in Igen cavern had no pride of place either, and any accommodation, transient or semipermanent, was marked by mute evidence of their occupancy.

The moons came out, bright Belior high and the smaller, dimmer Timor halfway down her arc, highlighting Igen River. Aramina wondered how long her father had planned this exodus, for not only did they have illumination but the river, dried by the summer's sun, was low enough to make crossing to the Lemos side relatively easy and safe. Very soon, when the fall rains began in the high mountains, no one would be able to cross the torrent that rampaged around the bend, flooding the now shallow ford. Aramina also remembered that Thella and Giron had been in the cavern that very afternoon, unlikely to return for several days, thus giving the fleeing family some margin of escape. Neither had approached Aramina, for which she had been *grateful*, but perhaps Thella had alarmed Dowell. Whatever the reason, Aramina was *grateful* on many counts to be away from the brawling, odorous, overcrowded cavern. And she knew that Barla would be, too. Her brother Pell's tendency to brag about his family would now be limited to hill and forest, wherry and tunnel snake.

The dray beasts were already hitched to the family's wagon, a smallish one but adequate for four people. Since Aramina heard dragons and could give warning of the imminence of Threadfall, the family could travel with some impunity. It was this talent, until just recently considered the family's most valuable asset, that the Lady Holdless Thella wished to pervert to her unlawful ends.

Aramina shifted her sleeping sister once more,

for both shoulders ached, and Nexa, like other inanimate objects, appeared to grow heavier. Pell had awakened; his initial outburst muffled by Dowell's large hand, he now trotted beside his father, burdened by the shawl bundle, and complained in a low undertone. Aramina came abreast of him.

"If you hadn't blabbed to show off, we wouldn't *be* running away," she said to him in a tone for his ears only.

"We aren't running," Pell snapped back, grunting as the shawl bundle cracked him on the right shin. "We don't run away. We change camps!" He was

taunting her now with her own words, used on previous occasions to ease the stigma of their holdlessness. "But where can we go," and his voice became a frightened wail, "that Thella can't find us?"

"It's me she wants, and she won't find me. You'll be safe."

"I don't want to be safe," Pell replied stoutly, "if you have to run because of me and my big mouth."

"Hush!" said Dowell in a sharp voice. The children trudged the rest of the way in silence.

Their dray beasts, Nudge and Shove, turned their heads, lowing softly at the approach of familiar people; Dowell had left them with sufficient grain in their feed bags to content them. Barla climbed into the rear of the hide-covered wagon, took the sleeping Nexa from Aramina, the bundle from Pell, and gestured the children to the fore where Dowell was untying ring reins from the tether stone. Aramina and Pell reclaimed their goods from the wagon and took their positions, one on either side of the team, ready to encourage them into the river and up the bank on the far side. Dowell and Barla would walk behind to push should the wagon founder.

Despite the hour and the circumstances of their departure, Aramina felt a tremendous relief as they moved off. Two Turns ago she had been inexpressibly relieved not to have to plod at the pace of Nudge and Shove day after weary day. But now traveling was a far more palatable alternative to being part of Thella's vindictive schemes.

"We are not holdless by choice, Aramina," Barla had often abjured her daughter, "for your father held well under Lord Kale of Ruatha Hold. Oh," and Barla would bow her head and press her hands to her mouth in anguish over terrible memories, "the perfidy, the treachery of that terrible, ruthless man! To murder all Ruatha blood in one pitiless hour!" Barla would gather herself then, lifting her head proudly. "Nor would your father serve Lord Fax of the High Reaches." Barla was not an extravagant person in word or deed, retaining a quiet and unobtrusive dignity despite all the slights and pettiness that came the way of the holdless. Her acrimony was therefore the more memorable, and Aramina, as well as her surviving brother and sister, knew Fax as the villain, despoiler, and tyrant, possessed of no single redeeming virtue. "We had pride enough to leave when he made his unspeakable order . . ." Barla would often color and then pale when reciting this part of their exodus. "Your father had made this very wagon for us to attend Gathers."

Barla would sigh. "Attend Gathers as respected holders, not as wanderers, holdless and friendless. For other Lord Holders did not wish to antagonize Fax just then, and though your father had been so certain of a welcome elsewhere, there was none. But we are *not* like the others, children. We chose to retain our honor and would not submit to the incarnate evil of Fax."

Although Barla would never be specific about that, of late Aramina was beginning to get glimmerings, now that she had become a woman. For Barla, despite the depredations of fourteen Turns of nomadic life and endless pregnancies as tokens of Dowell's esteem, still retained a beautiful face and a slender figure. Aramina was old enough to realize that Barla was far more handsome than most holdless women and that, when they entered a new hold, Barla kept her lustrous hair hidden under a tattered head scarf and wore the many-layered garments of cold poverty.

Dowell had been a skilled wood joiner, holding a modest but profitable hold for Lord Kale in the forests of Ruatha. News of the treacherous massacre of the entire bloodline had reached the mountain fastness long after the event, when a contingent of Fax's rough troops had thundered into the hold's yard and informed the astounded Dowell of the change in Lord Holder. He had bowed his head—reluctantly but wisely—to that announcement and kept his resentment and horror masked, hoping that none of the troop realized that his wife, Barla, expecting her first child, also bore Ruathan blood in her veins.

If Dowell hoped that a meek acceptance and an isolated location would keep him from Fax's notice, he erred. The leader of the troop had eyes in his head; if he couldn't detect Barla's bloodline at a glance, one look was enough to tell him that here was a woman of interest to Lord Fax. Nor had the man's shrewd gleam escaped Dowell, and the woodcrafter had made contingency plans, which began with leaving the hold's Gather wagon and two sturdy dray beasts in a blind valley on the Tillek side of the mountain. When half a Turn had passed with no further visitation, Dowell had begun to think his precautions foolish: that he had mistaken the man's reaction to Barla's beauty.

Then Lord Fax, followed by a score of his men, came galloping up the narrow trace to the woodland hold. His scowl had been frightening when he had seen Barla's gravid state.

"Well, the pump will be primed and ready. She'll

whelp soon. Collect her in two months. See that she is waiting for her Lord Holder's summons!"

Without a backward look, Fax had cruelly spun his runner about and, clouting the lathered creature with his rawhide whip, clattered back the way he had come.

Dowell and Barla had left their hold within the hour. Seven days later, a boy had been prematurely born, and died. Nor did Dowell and Barla find a ready sanctuary in Tillek's hold.

"Not this close to Fax, man. Perhaps farther west," their first host has suggested. "I don't want him knocking on my hold door. Not that one!"

Dowell and Barla had traveled ever since, to the western reach of Tillek, where they had found brief respites in their journeyings while Dowell carved bowls and cups or joined cabinets, or crafted Gather wagons. A few weeks here, a half Turn there; and Aramina was born on their way through the mountains of Fort, the first of Barla's children to survive birth. The news of Fax's death caught up with them in the vast plains of Keroon, just after Nexa's birth.

"Ruatha Hold brought Fax nothing but disease and trouble," the harper told Dowell and Barla in Keroonbeasthold, where Dowell was building stables.

"Then we could return and claim our hold again."

"If there's anything to claim. But I'm told that Lytol is a fair man and he'll need good workers," the harper had said, eyeing the notched timbers that Dowell had fitted.

"We'll return then," Dowell had told Barla, "when I've finished my bond with the mastercraftsman."

More than a full Turn later, they did begin the long journey up the Keroon peninsula, with a sturdy daughter, a small son, and a tiny baby.

Then Thread began to fall on the innocent green land, raining destruction on a population that had denied the existence of their ancient enemy. Once again dragons filled the skies with their fiery breath, charring the dread menace in midair, saving the rich land from the devouring Thread.

Travel became more hazardous than ever for the holdless; people clung to the safety of stone walls and stout doors, and to the traditional leadership of their Lord Holders. Within those sanctuaries there was little room for those without legitimate claim on leadership, supplies, and refuge. A new terror was visited on the unfortunate, deprived for any number of reasons of their right to hold or craft affiliation.

For Dowell and Barla, the terror was slightly abated by Aramina's unexpected ability to hear dragons. When she first naively reported such conversations, she had been soundly spanked for telling lies. Then came the day when she persisted in warning them that her dragons said Threadfall was imminent. Threatened with a second thrashing and a supperless night, she had tearfully refused to retract her report. It was only when Dowell saw the leading edge of Thread, a silver smudging in the sky, dotted with the fiery blossoms of dragon breath, that he had apologized. As the family lay crouched under a rocky ledge just large enough to shelter them, they were grateful to her.

"The lords of Ruatha have always given dragonriders complete hospitality," Barla had said, shielding the squalling Nexa against her shoulder. She had to stop to wipe grit from her lips. "No one in my immediate family was ever taken on Search, but then, there haven't been that many Searches in my lifetime. Aramina comes by her talent as a right of blood."

"And to think I ever complained that our first-born was female," Dowell had murmured, smiling at

Aramina, tucked in the safest angle of the rock ledge. "I wonder if Nexa will be able to hear dragons."

"I'll bet I will when I'm older," Pell had ventured, not wishing to let his sister take all the honors.

"It means we'll be safe traveling across Telgar Plains to Ruatha, for Aramina can always warn us about Threadfall. We won't need to be beholden to any lord for shelter!"

To be without restraint or obligation meant a great deal to Dowell's pride. Since the advent of Threadfall, the holdless had suffered more than the usual indignities at the hands of holders, large and small. Having no right of affiliation, they could be cheated of the ordinary rights of hospitality; overcharged for any goods their infrequent marks could purchase; forced to work unnatural hours for the mere privilege of shelter from Thread; deprived of dignity and honor; and, above all else, required to express gratitude for even the least condescension shown by holders and crafters.

The elation of the small family was short-lived, for their dray beasts had run off in the panic of Threadfall. Dowell was forced to return to Keroonbeasthold on foot, hire his skill at a hard-bargained price for the next Turn, then trudge all the way back with the new team to where his family had waited, fearful of marauding holdless men and women and Threadfall.

The indenture over, Dowell had once again turned team and wagon westward. A miscarriage and fever had forced them to take refuge in the huge Igen cave, and expediency had kept them there when Dowell's resolution had faltered under a series of misfortunes, all apparently designed to thwart his repatriation to Ruatha Hold.

Now they pushed on through the night, struggling to escape yet another threat to honor and resolve.

From somewhere Dowell had acquired a map of Lemos Hold, complete with road, track, and trace. Lemos had so many forests and mountains that rivers, Pern's other roadways, were unusable. Dowell elected to follow the faintest of tracks and was careful to remove any droppings. When he finally allowed them to rest, it was noontime. During the brief respite he allowed his family and team, Dowell crushed leaves and stained the wagon's leather cover with green to make it less visible to any searching eye.

"We'll be safe in the forests of Lemos," he said, reassuring himself as well as his family. "There are caves there in the mountains which no one could find. . . ."

"If no one can find them, how will we?" asked Pell reasonably.

"Because we'll be looking very hard, of course," Aramina answered before her weary father's short temper flared.

"Oh!"

"And we'll live by ourselves and thrive on the provender that woods naturally provide us," Aramina went on, "for we'll have all the wood we need to be warm, and nuts and roots because we know where to look for them, and berries and roast wherry . . ."

"Roast wherry?" Pell's eyes widened with delight at such a promise.

"Because you fashion such excellent snares . . ."

"I always caught more tunnel snakes than any one else at Igen," Pell began. Then, remembering that this helter-skelter trip was due to his boastfulness, he covered his mouth with his hand and huddled into a tight ball of remorse.

"Any of the forest caves ought to have lots of snakes, shouldn't they, Mother?" Aramina asked, wanting to lighten her mother's sad face as well as her brother's guilt.

"They should," Barla agreed in the absent way of parents who have not really attended to their children's conversation.

Dowell called them to order, and they continued on their way until Nudge refused to go farther and, when Dowell took the stick to him, sank resolutely to his knees. Unhitching the recalcitrant brute, they forced Shove to haul the wagon into the brush at the side of the trace.

"Nudge has got sense," Pell muttered to his sister as the weary children gathered enough branches to screen the wagon.

"Father has, too. I certainly didn't want to help Thella or," and Aramina shivered with revulsion, "that dragonless man, Giron."

"They're as bad as Fax."

"Worse."

Although Barla roused herself sufficiently to hand out dry rations, she found that Aramina and Pell had fallen asleep.

Only when they had put four mountains between themselves and Igen River did Dowell let up on the pace he had set. On the narrow traces, more logging tracks than proper trails, there were none to witness their passage as they climbed higher into the vast Lemos range.

They were not quite alone, for dragons passed overhead on daily sweeps and Aramina reveled in their conversations. She made her reports amusing, to liven evening campfire—for Dowell had conceded that a careful, smokeless fire would not be easily seen in the thick woods.

"It was green Path again today, with Heth and Monarth," Aramina said on the tenth day after their exodus from Igen Cave. "Lamanth, the queen, has clutched thirty fine eggs, but Monarth says that there are no queen eggs."

"There aren't always queen eggs," Dowell reminded Aramina, who sounded unhappy.

"That's what Path said. I don't know why Monarth was upset."

"I didn't realize that dragons talked to each other," Barla remarked, puzzled. "I thought they only talked to their riders."

"Oh, they do," Aramina assured her. "Heth talks constantly to K'van when they're doing the sweep alone."

"Why are there three today then?" Pell asked.

"Because Threadfall is imminent."

"Why didn't you say so?" Dowell wanted to know, exasperated with his daughter's diffidence.

"I was going to. They think Threadfall will come over Lemos tomorrow late afternoon."

"How can we survive Threadfall out in these woods?" Dowell demanded, angry with apprehension.

"You said there were lots of caves here in Lemos," Pell said, grimacing his face into a tearful expression.

"We'll need one!" Dowell said grimly. "We'll start first light tomorrow. Aramina, you and Pell will search ahead. On the upper slope. For there is bare cliff above us and somewhere there must be a cave for shelter."

"And we'll need more roots and anything else you can find to eat," Barla added, showing the empty stewpot as proof of the need. "There's naught left of the dried meat and vegetables."

"Why is it Thread always comes at times like these?" Pell asked, but expected no answer to his plaint.

He had occasion to repeat much the same expression the next morning when the off-rear wheel, sinking in a leaf-covered hole, cracked the cotter pin and lazily spun off. The team dragged the wagon on for several lengths, grinding the hub into the dirt before Dowell was able to halt them. Grimly he surveyed the damage. Then, with the sigh of long-suffering patience, he set to the job of repairing the wheel.

It was by no means the first time that wheels had come off, and Aramina and Pell needed no instructions to search out stout limbs, and to help roll a boulder into place for the lever. Indeed it was a well-drilled operation, and Aramina and Pell had wedged two blocks under the wagon bed as soon as Dowell and Barla had levered it up. They had the wheel back on the axle when Dowell discovered that there were no more cotter pins or kingpins in the wagon. He'd used the last on the journey to Igen Cave and had no reason to replace them in the long Turn.

"With the world and all of wood about us, Dowell?" Barla had remonstrated to cut short his flow of self-recriminations. "There's a hardwood over there. It can't take much time to whittle new pegs. The children can forage ahead for food and a cave. Come." She handed him the hatchet. "I'll help. Aramina, take a sack and one of the hide buckets. Pell, make one of your snares and set it if you cross snake spoor. Nexa, you may carry the small shovel, but don't lose it in the woods."

"If you hear more about Threadfall from the dragons, Aramina, you come back to me straightaway," Dowell added as he made for the hardwood visible from the track. "Don't dally."

With a spirit of urgent adventure the three children ran up the track. For the first four switchbacks, there was nothing but forest on either side, though Pell insisted on inspecting several outcroppings of the gray rock that he felt looked promising.

Then the logging trace started a long, straight run, which finally disappeared around a rocky outthrust. To their right, up a steep bank, the trees were sparser as the native rock intruded.

"I'll go look up there, 'Mina!" Pell cried, and took off just as Nexa called Aramina's attention to the unmistakable if withered tops of redroots growing on the downside.

Aramina saw Pell scrambling for footing on the steep and slippery bank, and elected to forage with Nexa. They had been digging for only a short while when Aramina heard Pell's warbling, the family signal for an emergency. Fearful that he had injured himself climbing, Aramina raced back to the track.

"I found a cave, 'Mina! I found a cave." Pell slithered back down the bank. "A good deep one. Room for Nudge and Shove, too." His voice reflected the jouncing his body took as he half walked, half slid the remaining distance to his sister.

"And lost your gathering," she said sternly, pointing to the cluster of broken bulge-nut twigs he still clutched in his left hand.

"Oh, them." Pell tossed the useless bits aside, stood up, and brushed the wet leaves from his leathern pants. "There're plenty more where they . . ." He broke off, an uncertain look on his face as his hand hesitated.

"Hmm, sprung the seams again, too," Aramina said impatiently and, grabbing him, swung him about to see the damage the slide had done his trousers. She sighed, controlling her temper. Pell never considered risk and consequence.

"Only the seam. Not the leather. Mother can mend it! In the cave I just found. Plenty of space." Grinning broadly to soothe the frown from his sister's face, he made exaggerated gestures with his arms, outlining the splendor of his discovery.

"How far up the slope?" Aramina regarded the steep incline with a thoughtful eye. "I'm not sure Nudge and Shove could make it."

"They'll make it 'cause there's grass and water . . ."

"The cave is damp?"

"Nah! Dry as far in as I went." Pell cocked his head sideways. "And I didn't go *all* the way in, just like you always warn me. Only far enough to see it was big and dry. And the tunnel snake signs. Good eating." He rolled his eyes and smacked his lips at the prospect. "There's even a stream and—a cascade, too."

Aramina hesitated, eyeing the steep bank and wondering if Pell's enthusiasm hadn't clouded his judgment. Pell would go through life seeing only what he hoped he was seeing, not what really was. But the need to get under shelter was critical. No matter if Pell had exaggerated: he had found a cave. Her father could decide on its suitability.

"How far up the slope is it?"

"Straight to the top of the ridge"—Pell pointed—"down into the dip past the nut plantation. Turn to your right at the forked birch and you'll stare right at the entrance. Only it's to the left. A good overhang. C'mon, I'll show you."

"No, you wait here. Nexa's down there digging roots"—Aramina pulled a face at her brother's sour expression—"which we need nearly as much as the cave." She hesitated once more. Maybe she ought to check the cave first, rather than raise false hopes.

"Ah, 'Mina, I wouldn't lie about shelter."

Aramina scrutinized her brother's face, his features contorted into an expression of utter trustworthiness. No, Pell wouldn't lie about something that important. A ray of sunlight broke through the clouds, lancing past the soughing tree branches, reminding her that there was little time left if they were to be under cover when Thread fell.

"*Don't* wander off! You know how scared Nexa gets." Aramina threw a deft twist of cord about the neck of her root sack and tossed it to the side of the logging track.

"I won't stir from her side. But I expect I'd do better gathering kindling." Thus avoiding his most hated chore of rooting, Pell diligently collected branches.

Aramina started off down the track in a lope, her long plaits bouncing off her shoulders and buttocks. She was light on her feet, moving with an economy of movement that would have been envied by a hold runner.

The sunlight seemed to follow her, illuminating her way on the overgrown trace, the springiness underfoot making the going a pleasure. She shortened her stride as the track switched back on itself, and listened intently, over the thud of her footfalls, for the sound of the wagon. Surely it hadn't taken her father too long to whittle the necessary pins: Dowell and Barla should have made some distance up the logging road. Surely she ought to have heard the lumbering wagon, her father's voice urging Nudge and Shove to their task.

Peering through the thickly planted trees, Aramina looked for some glimpse of the covered wagon. Apprehension lent her impetus and down the trace she sped, every nerve anxiously alert for any reassuring sight or sound. Faster she ran, positive now in her mind that something had happened. Could Lady Holdless Thella have possibly caught up with them?

Taking a more direct line, she bypassed the next turn and pushed through the underbrush, wiggling past trees. Then, as she discerned the bulk of the green-smeared wagon cover through the trees, she moved more circumspectly. The wagon had not shifted from the spot in which they had left it two hours past.

Trembling with fear, Aramina paused, listening now for the sound of voices, for the bass rumble of Giron or the crisp acid alto of Thella. Hearing nothing but the wind soughing through the leafless trees, she moved cautiously down until she was poised on the bank above where the wagon was still canted. Muffling a cry of fear, Aramina slid down the bank, recoiling in horror as she saw her father's head and shoulders protruding from under the wagon. Somehow the blocks had slipped and the wheel lay once again on its side. Horrified, Aramina was certain that her father had been crushed to death until she saw that one block had fallen directly under the wagon bed, preventing the complete collapse of the heavy load onto her father's chest.

Only then did Aramina hear the hoarse grunt and half sob, as she realized that her mother was attempting to lever the wagon bed off her stricken husband.

"Mother!"

"I cannot lift it, 'Mina!" Barla sobbed, leaning exhaustedly against the pole. "I've been trying and trying."

Wasting no words, Aramina threw her weight onto the lever, and though Barla gave every remaining ounce of her strength, the two women could not summon enough mass between them to shift the wagon more than a finger's breadth.

"Oh, 'Mina, what can we do? Even if we had Pell and Nexa, they couldn't help enough. . . ." Defeated, Barla slumped onto the ground, weeping.

"*We* lifted it enough. If Pell and Nexa were here, they could pull him free. . . ." Aramina swung 'round to her father, his tanned face pale with shock, the pulse in his neck beating slowly but reassuringly. "Pell's found a cave. It's not too far up the track. I'll be right back."

Giving Barla no chance to protest, Aramina started up the track again as fast as she could run. Pell and Nexa just *had* to be strong enough. She

didn't dare believe anything else. And they must hurry. The sun glancing into her eyes warned her that time was very short if they were to rescue Dowell and get the wagon up the trail to the cave. She couldn't consider any other problems then, only the most immediate ones, and she almost ignored

the sight of the dragon gliding overhead. She stopped so fast that she almost fell.

Dragon, dragon, hear me! Help me! HELP ME! Aramina had never attempted to communicate with the dragons, but a dragonrider would be strong enough to help her. Surely a dragonrider would not ignore her need.

Who calls a dragon?

She recognized the voice of Heth.

It is Aramina. Down on the logging trace, above the river in the forest. Please help me. My father is trapped beneath our wagon. And Thread will fall soon! She jumped up and down in the middle of the trace, waving frantically. *Oh, please help me!*

No need to shout. I heard you the first time. My rider wants to know who you are.

To her relief, Aramina saw the dragon change directions, circling down toward the track.

I told you, I'm Aramina.

May I tell him?

Such consideration rarely came Aramina's way.

Yes, yes, of course. Are you Heth?

I am Heth. My rider is K'van.

How do you do?

I'd do better if we could see you.

But I'm right here. In the middle of the trace. And the wagon is large. . . . Oh, my father painted it green. If you'll just fly lower . . .

I'm a dragon, not a wherry. . . . K'van sees the wagon.

Aramina crashed through the underbrush to reach the wagon at the same time as dragon and rider. Barla looked about to faint with shock at their sudden appearance.

"It's all right, Mother. They'll help us. They're much stronger than Pell and Nexa would be." Then Aramina realized that Shove and Nudge were taking great exception to the proximity of a dragon. She tied them tightly down by their nose rings to the tether stone, giving them more immediate pain to occupy their stupid brains.

Fortunately, the dragonrider directed Heth to land behind the wagon, out of the dray beasts' immediate sight.

To her dismay, Aramina realized that both dragon and rider were young. She'd always thought that bronze dragons must be big, and, indeed, Heth had seemed enormous, outlined in the sky. But now she could see that he wasn't fully grown and that his rider, K'van, was both undersized and younger than herself.

As if K'van sensed her disappointed appraisal, he straightened his shoulders and jerked his chin up. He walked forward, taking in the lever propped against the boulder and looking down at the prostrate Dowell.

"We may be weyrlings, but we can help you," K'van said without ostentation. He turned to Heth. "What I want you to do is to put heave on this, Heth, with your forearms. C'mon, Aramina."

Aramina stopped staring at the bronze dragon,

who waddled forward to place his five-clawed paws about the lever.

"Not until I say go, Heth," K'van cautioned, grinning a bit at Aramina as they knelt in the dust beside the unconscious Dowell, fastening their hands under the man's armpits. "Heave, Heth! Heave!"

As quickly as they could, Aramina and K'van hauled Dowell's body from under the wagon. With a cry of incredulous relief, Barla rushed to her husband's side, opening his shirt to judge the extent of his injury. K'van had the presence of mind to replace the fallen block and prop the wagon up.

"You'll need the wheel back on," he said to Aramina. "That was fine, Heth."

I am very strong, said the dragon with a trace of smugness, his great faceted eyes whirling bluey green as he maintained pressure on the lever.

"Oh, you are indeed, you beautiful, beautiful creature," cried Aramina.

"All right, Heth, ease it down," said K'van, holding the block in place. "Slowly now."

The wagon settled, creaking as the block took its weight. K'van fumbled about in the grass and dust and triumphantly held up the pegs.

"Mother?" Aramina's trembling voice held a question as she turned to look at her father.

"I can't find anything broken," Barla said in a low unsteady voice, "but look . . ." Her hand indicated the terrible line of bruising already discoloring the skin. Carefully she smoothed the hair back from Dowell's brow, her expression of concerned tenderness causing the two young people to exchange embarrassed glances.

K'van touched Aramina's arm. "Do you know how to set the wheel back on the axle?" He gave her a rueful glance as he proffered the pegs. "I don't."

"Whyever should you?" Aramina wanted to know as she took the pegs and noticed, with a pang, how carefully Dowell had made a cotter hole in the kingpin. "You're a dragonrider."

"Not all that long," he said with a grin as he helped her lift the wheel and roll it into position. "And weyrlings are taught a little bit of every craft needed by the Weyr. You never know when something will come in handy. Like now!" He said this on the end of a grunt as the two young people tried to force the wheel onto the axle.

"It's the dirt encrusted on the hub," Aramina said as K'van paused uncertainly. With her belt knife, she scraped off the caked dirt, found a large rock, and, with a healthy knock, set the wheel firmly on. With another few taps of her rock, she rammed the kingpin through and then the cotter pin into its place.

"You're deft at that," K'van said admiringly.

"Practice."

With Heth's assistance, they removed the block from under the wagon.

"Have you far to go?" K'van asked then. "Thread falls soon and, as I recall, the foresters' hold is a long ways up the track."

Barla stifled a sound in her throat, but Aramina had an answer ready.

"I know," Aramina lied calmly, "but this accident delayed us. However, there's a cave not far up the track where we can wait out Threadfall."

"Is it large?" asked K'van.

"Large enough. Why?" Aramina asked, suddenly wary.

"Well, just before you called us," and K'van grinned ingenuously for her temerity, "Heth spotted a band of runners beyond the river. Are they part of your group?"

"No." Barla groaned aloud, looking wildly up at Aramina.

"There shouldn't be anyone else in this part of Lord Asgenar's forests," Aramina said with all the indignation she could muster. "We were warned that holdless raiders have been seen."

"Holdless men?" K'van was instantly alert. "If they are, they'll disperse once they've seen me. Look, let me help you get your father into the wagon and see you safely on your way to the cave. I'll take care of the raiders. And warn Lord Asgenar, too."

Aramina hadn't expected that, but she said what was appropriate, determined to play out her part in this charade. She unfastened the tailgate so that they could slide Dowell in. Then, while K'van watched beside Heth, she and Barla took up their positions and prodded Nudge and Shove into a walk, and then into a shambling trot up the trace.

Barla and Aramina had to keep hard at the dray beasts to maintain their trot. Nudge resented the pace, twisting his horned head and lowing piteously, but Aramina had no mercy on him. Women and beasts were sweating when they finally reached the bank, Pell cheering lustily until Aramina shouted at him to stop being so foolish and come help.

In a few terse words, Aramina explained what had happened, and Pell began shaking his head slowly from side to side.

"I don't know how we'll get Father up that bank," he said, appraising the difficulty. "You shouldn't've sent the dragonrider away."

"It's not just Father being hurt, Pell. K'van saw a troop of riders on the other side of the river...."

Pell quailed, and his distress communicated itself to Nexa, who had been standing there, wide-eyed and perplexed. Now she burst into tears.

"So we must also get the wagon out of sight. And hide Nudge and Shove."

"But Thread's coming. And we have to get Father up to the cave and ..." Pell's words tripped over themselves in his anxiety.

"Somehow we'll do it," Aramina said, peering up and down the trace to find a possible screen for the mass of the wagon. "Maybe, if K'van has frightened them with Threadfall, they'll have to go back the way they came. ... Maybe if we rig a stretcher, we can haul Father up the bank. ..."

"Maybe, maybe, *maybe!*" Pell almost danced with frustration.

"I won't have you children fighting at a time like this," Barla said tartly, appearing in the back of the wagon. "We've got to rouse your father. ... How long before Thread falls, Aramina? Or didn't you ask the dragonrider?"

Aramina bowed her head at her mother's rebuke. As she did so, her glance fell on a group of evergreens on the left-hand side of the roadway a few lengths farther up the track.

"There!" she cried dramatically, gesturing wildly. "There! We can drive the wagon in there, behind the evergreens. They're just tall enough!"

With something constructive to do, even Nexa

stopped her whingeing. Dowell was carefully lifted out of the wagon and covered by a sleeping fur. Then everyone concentrated on getting the wagon out of sight. Nexa was directed to brush away the tracks of the wagon as Aramina and Pell forced the dray beasts through the opening Barla parted into the copse. The artistic addition of extra branches completed the camouflage.

Then Barla sent Pell and Nexa on ahead to the cave with sleeping furs and Barla's precious stewpot, while Aramina and her mother tried to rouse Dowell. The usual aromatic had no effect, and the two women exchanged anxious glances, when suddenly Nudge and Shove, tethered by the trace, began to moan fearfully and pull at their ring ropes.

"Thread?" gasped Barla, bending protectively over her husband.

"No," cried Aramina, "Dragons! *Big* dragons!" Indeed it seemed to her as if the sky was filled with them, their great wings causing the saplings to bend to their backwind.

"Aramina, *how* did that dragonrider come to help us in the first place? You didn't *call* him, did you?" When Aramina mutely nodded, Barla gave a despairing cry. "But the Weyrs will take you from us if they know you can hear and speak to dragons! And then what shall we do?"

"How else were we to save Father?" asked Aramina even as she, too, regretted her action.

I hear Aramina, said Heth's unmistakable voice.

Oh, please go away, Heth. Say you can't find me.

But I have! You must not fear. We won't harm you. Before Aramina could speak again, three dragons skimmed neatly down onto the track, making Nudge and Shove buck and strain to be free of their tether. As one, Barla and Aramina dashed forward to prevent the escape of the dray beasts, twisting the nose rings until pain paralyzed the stupid animals.

We will move down the track, Aramina heard Heth say as she coped with the frantic Nudge. When the dragons were far enough away not to be an immediate threat, Aramina and Barla relaxed their hold.

"I am T'gellan, bronze rider of Monarth, and this is Mirrim, who rides green Path," said the oldest of the three riders who approached them. "K'van wisely called for help to persuade those holdless raiders to absent themselves from this vicinity. So I thought we'd better make sure you had safely reached shelter before Threadfall."

Barla hovered between her critical need for assistance and anxiety at the presence of dragonriders who might very easily depart with her daughter who could hear dragons.

Mirrim knelt beside Dowell and opened his shirt, then exhaled her breath on a long whistle.

"I can feel no broken bones, but he's not regained consciousness," Barla told Mirrim, sensibly making her husband's needs her first priority.

"If he was under a wagon as K'van says, that doesn't surprise me," Mirrim remarked. "I've done considerable nursing at the Weyr. First let's get him to this cave."

"We don't have much time to spare," T'gellan added, squinting at the steep bank. "And I don't fancy trying to haul an unconscious man up that!"

"Is there any sort of a clearing by your cave?" Mirrim asked Aramina.

"A small one," she said, devoutly hoping that Pell's description bore some resemblance to fact.

"Path? Would you oblige us?" Mirrim asked the green dragon.

I see no reason why not. In a maneuver that Aramina couldn't believe she was seeing, the green dragon glided to the group without moving her wings or appearing to walk. *Silly beasts, aren't they?* Path added as Nudge and Shove began their terrified lowing again.

Aramina was obliged to go calm them; their perturbation abruptly ceased as Mirrim, Path, her father, and her mother disappeared.

"Well, it seemed easier to send your mother along, too, Aramina," T'gellan said with a laugh for her astonishment. "You'd best go the hard way. Thread will fall very shortly."

"But I can't . . . Nudge and Shove . . ."

K'van grinned. "Just get on one, get a good hold on the nose rein of the other. We'll supply the impulsion." And he jerked his thumb at the two dragons watching with their jewel eyes whirling mildly.

It was perhaps the wildest ride Aramina had ever had. In the first place, dray beasts were not designed for comfortable riding, having straight backs, wide withers, short necks and low-held heads. However, the flapping of dragon wings behind Nudge and Shove was more than enough to have sent them plunging through fire. They took the bank, cloven hooves slipping on the wet footing in no more than four bucking jumps. Momentum carried them over the top and down the dip, almost right into the cliff wall, where they fetched up to a dead stop that sent Aramina onto Nudge's horns, and then to the ground with a force that jarred her from heel to headbones.

Pell appeared, eyes wide at her impetuous arrival.

"A girl on a green dragon brought Father and Mother. I didn't think girls were allowed to ride fighting dragons."

"Help me get these inside the cave before they stampede again," Aramina said, though she had been equally surprised by Mirrim and Path.

"Oh, look, they're going!" Pell's disappointment was patent, as he saw the dragons hover briefly in the sky. "I'm forever missing the good parts," he complained.

"Get Shove inside!" Aramina had no time to humor her brother, and she gave him such a hard prod that he sharply reminded her that he wasn't any old dray beast.

He hauled on the nose rein and, lowing, Shove followed his painful muzzle—then bellowed as his hindquarters scraped along the right wall of the narrow entry. Aramina pushed at his dappled flanks and set him right. She was careful to line Nudge squarely in the opening, and to prevent any further recalcitrance she twisted his nose ring. With an injured bellow, he, too, made the passage into the cave, running into Aramina, who stopped, amazed at what lay before her.

"Isn't this cave marvelous, 'Mina? Didn't I find a

good one? Couldn't we get everything in here? Maybe we could even live here." Pell dropped his voice to a hoarse whisper on the last sentence. "For it's as big as a hold, isn't it, 'Mina?" The boy was all but dancing at the end of Shove's ring rein, momentarily oblivious of everything but his need for her approval.

In a sweeping glance, Aramina saw a solemn-faced Nexa cradling her father's head where he lay on the pile of sleeping furs, and her mother busy lighting a small fire within a ring of stones before she allowed herself to examine the cave in more detail.

"Why, it is truly big enough to be a hold," she said in a voice awed enough to delight her brother.

"It's bigger than many holds we've been in, 'Mina," Pell said with great satisfaction. "Much bigger. It's nearly as big as any of the Igen caverns I ever was in."

Aramina appraised the high ceiling, dry as far as she could see in the dim light filtering in from the entrance. She could sense rather than see clearly that the cave extended far beyond the immediate chamber in which they stood.

"There's even a sort of stall place where we can

tether Nudge and Shove," he went on, babbling happily, and pulled on Shove to lead the way.

The beasts settled, Aramina and Pell came back to the front of the cavern, where Barla was coaxing the flames on the small hearth. Then a soft moan broke the silence as Dowell rolled his head from side to side in Nexa's lap. She snatched her hands away from him, as if contact might somehow impede his recovery. With startled eyes she looked about for reassurance.

"There now, Nexa, I told you he'd come around," said Barla, rising from the now healthy fire. "Aramina, we'll need fresh water. As cold as you can draw it. We've nothing but cold compresses to ease the bruising. And hurry. Those dragonriders said that Threadfall was a matter of minutes away."

" 'Mina," and Pell caught the other side of the bucket, accompanying his sister out of the cavern, "can you hear 'em yet?"

Aramina halted at the entrance, listening with every fiber in her ears, smiled at Pell, and walked quickly out.

"Show me where the water is," she said, and Pell danced around in front of her and to their left.

"Right here! Right here!" he caroled, pointing

and dancing about. "Just like I said. You won't ever doubt me again, will you, 'Mina?"

"No, I won't," she said, smiling as she extended her hand into the little cascade that leaped and fell down the side of the mountain. The water was ice cold, numbing her fingers in seconds. She filled the bucket. She was just at the entrance to the cave when Pell let out an excited whoop. At the same time she heard a multitude of voices, excited and anticipatory.

"They're here! I can see them! I saw them first!" His triumph found a lack in her talent.

"Well, I can hear them talking!"

"Can I watch the dragons fight Thread *this* time, 'Mina? This time can I watch?"

Aramina shushed him, examining the overhang of the cavern. Unless Thread should happen to fall at a tremendous velocity and at a slant, she couldn't see how any of the dreaded menace could score them. Turns of familiarity with Thread had dampened her fear of it.

"Yes, I think it's safe here for us to watch." She placed a warning finger on her lips, and, slipping quickly inside to bring her mother the bucket of cold water, she rejoined him in the entrance.

To Pell's keen disappointment, there wasn't as much to watch as he'd anticipated. They could see the dragons in their ranks, suspended motionless in the clear mountain air, gleaming where wing and body reflected the sun briefly. Then the two watching children saw the sudden blurring of the sky, the silvery mist that was the leading edge of Thread.

Only then did the dragons break the temporary suspension, swooping up to meet the deadly rain, sending blossoms of fiery breath to char the parasitic Thread. Pell didn't breathe with the wonder of the darting forays of the smaller dragons, exclaiming as he saw a long tongue of flame reach out to char a mass of Thread. Silver mist turned to black smoke and then dissipated lazily. Fire blooms traced the dragons' progress after their ancient enemy until the hills and trees covered the distant sight from the watchers' searching eyes.

"It didn't last long enough," Pell said dejectedly.

"It'll last long enough for the dragonriders, I'm sure," Aramina said with mild rebuke for his callousness. "Did you remember to bring the roots with you?"

"Ah, who wants to eat roots. There are acres of nuts out there."

"Then you'll have no trouble filling a sack, will you?" As Aramina turned back to the fire, she heard her father's querulous voice.

"I don't understand how you managed, with just Aramina."

"Pell was a great help, too," Barla said soothingly, wringing out another cold compress. She gave Aramina a quick stern glance.

"It was really very simple, Father. You keep telling us that if there was a lever long enough, we could even move Pern away from the Red Star," Aramina said with a smile.

"This is no time for levity," Barla said severely.

"Whyever not? Father's conscious, we've got this huge big cave all to ourselves, and Pell's gone out for more of these delicious nuts." Expertly Aramina positioned two in her palm and cracked them. "See?" She held out the meats to Barla.

After a supper of boiled roots and crisp nut-meats, Aramina and Pell used the last of the daylight to gather fodder for Nudge and Shove, and sufficient boughs and fragrant bracken for bedding.

Tired as she was, Aramina found that sleep eluded her. She had been brought up to honor truth, and today that teaching had been disregarded for expediency. She had permitted K'van to think that they were proper holders, on their lord's business. She had avoided truth with her father, although at Barla's behest, so as not to worry him.

In each case the truth would confound her lies in very short order. But . . . K'van had chased off the Lady Holdless Thella and the band that had nearly caught up with her and her family. And . . . they had contrived to get Dowell safely into this cave refuge, hopefully without leaving an easy trail that Thella could follow. But . . . to achieve that end, she had revealed her ability to hear dragons to Benden Weyr riders. And . . . the dragonriders now knew exactly where she was even if Lady Holdless Thella did not. She could not imagine what punishment would be meted out to her for that daylong imprudence.

Nexa, curled close against her sister's body, whimpered in a restless sleep. Aramina pulled the sleeping rug closely about her, stroking her arm, and Nexa subsided into sleep. For a while, she was distracted by Dowell's breathing, a light snore because he had to sleep on his back, but its soft rhythm finally lulled Aramina to sleep.

It seemed all too short a time before Pell was urgently tugging at her shoulders and whispering excitedly in her ear.

" 'Mina! 'Mina! K'van is here! And so is the Weyrleader! He wants to speak to you! And there are lots of strange men out there, too."

"Here?" Frantically brushing sleep from her eyes,

Aramina sat up, all too aware of yesterday's bruises and scrapes and the dull ache across her shoulders from abused muscles.

"No, on the track. The men are armed with bows and arrows and spears and I think the dragons brought them." Pell's eyes were wide with excitement. K'van was just beyond him.

"It's all right, Aramina, really it is," said K'van, softly so as not to disturb the other sleepers. "It's the raiders, you see."

Careful not to rouse Nexa, Aramina slipped out from under the fur and pressed it gently down about her sister.

"The raiders are coming?" Pell's voice slipped from whisper to harsh alarm, but Aramina quickly covered his mouth. Fear darkened his eyes as he stared at his sister.

The little one is suddenly afraid, said a surprised, richly mellow voice.

She has more to fear from the holdless. The second dragon voice was deep and dark, like a pool of the blackwater that Aramina had seen in Igen.

"I am *not* afraid of you." Aramina spoke stoutly.

"Of me?" K'van asked in astonishment, his hand on his chest.

"Not you. Those dragons." No, Aramina told

herself, she was not afraid of the dragons, but of their riders and the impending justice that would be meted out for all the lies of yesterday. She hoped that K'van would not think too badly of her.

"I don't think badly of you," K'van protested as they stepped out into the sunlight. "Why should I? I think you were an absolute marvel yesterday, fixing that wheel and getting everyone safe inside the cave...."

"Oh, you don't understand," said Aramina, trying to keep her voice from breaking.

"And neither does Heth but ..."

It will come right, said Heth as if he meant it.

Then they were at the top of the bank and Aramina held on to a sapling to steady herself at the sight of masses of armed men, just as Pell had reported, and an incredible stream of dragons, taking off and landing in the track. Standing slightly apart with the enormous bronze dragon and a brown almost as big was the Weyrleader, F'lar, and his wingleader, F'nor, talking earnestly with two men dressed in gleaming mail. A fur-trimmed cape was slung negligently over the shoulders of the younger man.

"Are those who I think they are?" asked Pell in an awed whisper. His hands clasped in his sister's arm for reassurance. Then he stiffened, for F'nor had seen the three standing on the bank. He smiled and beckoned them down.

Aramina prayed earnestly that she wouldn't lose her footing and arrive in an ignominious heap at the bottom of the slope. Then she felt K'van's steadying hand. It was Pell who slipped, tumbling almost to the feet of the Weyrleader, who, with an easy laugh, gave him a hand to his feet. Then Aramina and K'van reached the group.

"How is your father today?" F'lar asked with a sympathetic smile.

"Badly bruised but sleeping, Lord F'lar," Aramina managed to stammer. That was the correct form of address for the Weyrleader of Pern, wasn't it? Aramina braced herself for the worst.

"We'll hope not to disturb him, but those hold-less marauders did not disperse after Threadfall." F'lar's slight frown indicated his annoyance with that intransigence.

"So," F'nor took up the explanation, "Lord Asgenar plans to disperse them." He grinned as he gestured to the tall man.

It was all Aramina could do to stand straight as she stared, appalled to be in the company of the Lord Holder whose land had been invaded by impudent holdless raiders in pursuit of a trespassing holdless family. In a daze she heard Lord Asgenar wondering why the raiders were pressing so far into his forestry. She saw that men were marching down the track, quietly but in good array.

"I've foresters in the top camp, although I cannot see what profit raiders could make of sawn logs," Lord Asgenar was saying.

Now the truth must out, to save good men from Lady Holdless Thella's brutal riders.

"It's me."

Aramina's voice cracked so that her tentative admission was almost unheard. But the bronze dragon rumbled, and suddenly F'lar was regarding her with a sharp and penetrating gaze.

"You said that it was you, Aramina?"

The two men turned to gaze down at her. Pell's fingers tightened about her arm.

You do not need to fear, child.

"Mnementh's quite right, Aramina. Would you explain?"

"It's me. Because I can hear dragons. And the Lady Holdless Thella . . ."

"Thella, is it?" exclaimed Lord Asgenar, slapping his hand onto his sword hilt. "By the first egg, I've been longing to meet that one."

"Thella has been chasing you, child?"

ARAMINA

It was such a relief to admit to the first truth that her confession was almost incoherent, except that between her words Aramina kept hearing the reassurances of three dragon voices in her head, calming her, bidding her speak more slowly and above all not to be worried about a thing.

"So, Thella thinks to Search for what is the Weyr's by right?" F'lar's amber eyes flashed with a fire no less frightening than dragon breath. "And you and your family left Igen Cave only ten days ago? You have traveled hard to escape that woman. Where did you come from?"

"Last Turn my father bonded himself to Keroonbeastmaster. . . ."

"Then you are Keronese?"

"No, Lord F'lar. My father and mother had a small forest hold in Ruatha . . ."

Aramina stopped in midsentence, startled by the play of surprise and comprehension that flashed across the faces of the dragonriders.

"Lessa should have come, after all, F'lar," F'nor said, grinning with some private amusement at the Weyrleader.

"So Fax made your family holdless, Aramina."
F'lar's voice was kind, though his eyes still sparkled.

Unable to speak, Aramina nodded.

"And your father was a forester?" Lord Asgenar's
question was eager.

Again Aramina could only nod.

"He's the best wood joiner and carver in all
Pern," Pell spoke up, sensing a sympathy in their audience that Aramina, immersed in guilt, could not
appreciate.

"Is he now? I thought as much." F'lar took up the
conversation, giving Aramina a chance to regain her
poise. "That's a very well made Gather wagon you hide
so neatly. We almost didn't spot it, did we, Asgenar?"

"Well hidden indeed. But I must go on, F'lar,
F'nor. My men are assembled. I'm leaving men to
guard your cave, Aramina, so you will have ab-
solutely nothing to fear from our Lady Holdless
Thella. Not now or again. We'll see to that."

And, at his signal, two men ranged behind
Aramina, K'van, and Pell. As Aramina watched the
tall young Lord Holder stride down the track to join
his men, she began to feel secure for the first time
since her first encounter with Thella and Giron.

"We must leave, too," F'lar said to F'nor. "Can't
let them sight dragons in the sky near this moun-

tain. Aramina. K'van brings some medicines for your father from our healer."

"We do not like to be beholden to anyone," Aramina replied, as her parents had drilled her to say to any such well-meant offers. "We have all we need with us." She caught her lip to be telling yet another untruth.

"But we,"—and F'lar bowed slightly toward her—"are beholden to you for luring that hellion Thella near enough to grab her."

"Oh!"

"Take the medicines, child. Ease your father's injuries," said F'nor, clasping Aramina's shoulders in his warm, gentle hands. He gave her a kindly little squeeze. "And don't be afraid."

"I'm not afraid," Aramina replied, for she wasn't. Not of the weyrmen. But what would her proud father say of her actions over the past two days?

Then both dragonriders quickly vaulted to their waiting dragons, swinging nimbly up onto the neck ridges. With mighty leaps that sent dust, pebbles, and bruised leaves flying, the two beasts launched themselves upward. Suddenly the trace was empty of dragons and men, and only the two soldiers and the youngsters remained to hear the morning breeze sighing through the forest.

"I wonder if they'd have taken me along to see Thella get trounced," Pell said, cocking his head around and beaming at the soldiers.

"Well now, lad, you should have asked, shouldn't you?" said the older guard. "Now, young lady, if you'll just lead the way to this cave of yours . . ."

"K'van, where's Heth got to? You're here. Where's he?" Pell wanted to know, looking all about him as if the bronze dragon might be roosting in a nearby tree.

"He's up at the cave, Pell. Probably asleep in that small clearing . . . if it's big enough. Dragons like the sun and we had a very busy day yesterday."

"And a busy one so far today, too," Pell said amiably, digging his toes into the damp mulch of the bank.

"You could do with some steps cut in this bank," said the younger soldier, who had just slipped as far as he had come.

"Oh, we couldn't do that," Pell replied, horrified. "We don't really live in that cave. Though I'd sure like to," he added with such ingenuousness that the older guard chuckled. "Can you make a good snare?" he asked him. " 'Cause that cave is just crawling with tunnel snakes. They'd make mighty good eating after months and months of nothing but roots and fish."

"I tie a pretty good snare," K'van said, grabbing a sapling to pull himself onto the top of the ridge.

"You? But you're a dragonrider."

"I wasn't always," K'van admitted, grinning over Pell's head at Aramina. "*Before* I was a dragonrider I was a very lowly weyrboy, and small. Just the right size to set snares for tunnel snakes. My foster mother used to give an eighth of a mark for every fifty snakes we caught."

"Really?" Pell was awed by the thought of riches beyond the eating. "Well," and Pell recovered from his awe, "I'm bloody good at snake-snaring, too, aren't I, Aramina?"

"Not if you use the word 'bloody' you aren't," she said in reproof, not wishing the soldiers to think that the holdless were also mannerless.

They had reached the clearing—and there was Heth, curled in a tight ball that just fit in the available space. The soldiers grinned as Pell, eyes wide, carefully circled the sleeping bronze dragon.

"The cave is where, young lady?" asked the guard leader.

Aramina pointed. "There!"

"There's water just to the right," Pell said hospitably, "and there's a whole grove of nuts just beyond the copse if you're hungry."

"Thank'ee, lad, we've rations with us." The guard patted a bulging pouch. "Though a drink of cold water would be welcome. Traveling *between* sort of dries a man's mouth of spit. You go on in, tell your folks not to worry. We'll be out here on guard."

"I'd rather stay with you," Pell said confidentially.

Aramina caught the guard's expression and hastily vetoed that option.

"Aw, Aramina, you had all the fun yesterday."

"Fun?" Aramina got a firm grip on his arm and pulled him ruthlessly toward the cave entrance.

"Later, perhaps, Pell," K'van said in the role of conciliator, "after you've eaten your breakfast, for I know I woke you out of a sound sleep. I've got enough *klah* here to serve everyone, and some bread, because Mende knew you wouldn't have had a chance to bake yesterday." K'van's engaging grin dared Aramina to reject the treats.

"Bread? *Klah?* What else do you have in that sack, K'van?" Pell, displaying the manners of the worst Igen holdless riffraff, tried to pull open the neck of the sack for a glimpse of its contents.

"Pell!" Aramina's shocked whisper reminded her brother of their sleeping parents as well as his manners.

"But, 'Mina, do you know how long it is since we had *klah*?"

"I've promised to make it for the guards, 'Mina," K'van said in a voice that had brought many around to indulge his whimsies. "Surely a cup between friends . . ."

She relented, though she was sure to receive a scolding on that account as well as for her other errors. But a cup of *klah* would do much to ease the trembling in her stomach and knees, and give her the energy to bear whatever other shocks this day might hold for her.

The aroma, as it steeped, roused the sleepers, though Barla's first conscious act was to peer in her husband's face, reassured by the soft snores that emanated from his slightly open mouth. Only then did Barla react to the fragrance of the brewing *klah*.

"We had no *klah*," she said, frowning at Aramina before she recognized K'van beside the little hearth.

"My foster mother, Mende, sent it along with fellis and numbweed salve to ease your husband's injury," said K'van, rising to bring her a cup of the fresh brew. He smiled with a shy charm to which Barla was scarcely impervious.

Aramina regarded the young bronze rider with astonishment.

"My Weyrleaders insisted that I return to see if he is recovering from the accident."

"That is kind of you, young K'van, but unnecessary. We do not care to be beholden to anyone." Barla pretended not to see the cup he offered, but Aramina saw her mother's nostrils twitch in appreciation of the aromatic steam.

K'van gave her another of his charming smiles. "I'm weyr-bred, you know," he said, undaunted, "so I know how you feel about being under obligation." When he saw Barla's incredulous expression, he went on. "Before the Pass began, Benden Weyr was begrudged every jot and tittle ... because"—and now his voice became querulous and his eyes took on a merry twinkle for his impersonation—"everyone knows that Thread won't fall on Pern again!" He grinned impishly at Barla's astonishment and her sudden realization that Benden had indeed once been relegated to a state not much different from that of the holdless: tolerated when unavoidable, ignored when possible, and condemned on every occasion for uselessness. "Drink, good lady, and enjoy it. Mende also sent along bread, knowing you'd've had no chance to bake yesterday."

"Mother, could we not send Mende one of the

wooden spoons Father carved at Igen?" Aramina
ventured to suggest to salve her mother's sensibility.

"Yes, an exchange is always permissible," Barla
replied and, inclining her head graciously, finally ac-
cepted the cup of *klah*.

Relieved by her mother's capitulation, Aramina
carefully cut a thick slice of the round loaf, spreading it generously with the jam that K'van had also
extracted from his sack of surprises. She bent a
stern glance on Pell when he started to devour the
treat ravenously.

Only when she had served the others did Aramina eat, savoring the *klah* and the thick, crunchy
bread spread with the berry jam. Daintily she
even rescued the crumbs from her lap with a moistened fingertip. When K'van and Pell went outside
to serve the guards, Barla summoned Aramina to the
sleeping furs, where she was delicately smearing
numbweed salve on the livid bruises on Dowell's
chest.

"Why is that rider still here?"

"He came back this morning, Mother." Then
Aramina took a deep breath, realizing that only the
truth would serve. Evasion was as dishonest as lying,
whatever her motive. The presence of the dragonriders and Lord Asgenar would ensure the safety of

everyone. With complete candor she accounted for her part in the events of the past day and this morning. "And the Benden Weyrleader was just here with Lord Asgenar and his men because Lady Holdless Thella *has* followed us. Lord Asgenar is using this opportunity to ambush her and that horrid band of hers. So we'll be safe now because Lord Asgenar and Lord F'lar think father built a fine Gather wagon. And truly, they did call it a Gather wagon just as if that's all it ever has been."

"That's what it was made for," said Dowell in a sad voice, slightly shaken by the pain of the shallow breaths he took to speak.

"Here, Dowell. Drink this fellis," Barla said, raising the carved wooden cup to his lips.

"Fellis? We had no fellis!"

"We have it now, Dowell. Don't be so proud it hurts!" Barla said, suspending pride in the interests of healing her husband.

Thus abjured, Dowell swallowed the dose, closing his eyes at the pain even that minor movement caused his swollen flesh.

Barla saw Aramina's tender concern. "The numbweed will be taking effect soon. I am truly grateful to this Mende. I think a spoon and one of the sandstone bowls. A woman can never have too many of them." She sighed. "I am truly grateful to her. And . . ." She turned to Dowell, who had closed his eyes in tacit accord. "I think that we must be grateful to you, daughter . . . in spite of the fact that you seem to have forgotten all we have tried to instill in you of manners and conduct."

Aramina bowed her head, assuming a contrite pose. Then she realized that although her mother's voice was sharp, there was no bite to her words. Discipline required a scolding, but this time it was only the form that was obeyed, not the spirit. Aramina looked up and tried not to smile at this unexpected absolution.

" 'Mina, if Lord Asgenar . . . ," Dowell began in a voice no stronger than a whisper, speaking in short phrases between the shallow breaths he took, ". . . favors us . . . with his presence again . . . we must request . . . formal permission to stay . . . in this cave . . . until I am able . . . to continue our journey."

"I'll tell him. And I'll mention it to the guard as well."

Dowell nodded again, closing his eyes, his mouth beginning to relax a little as fellis and numbweed gave him surcease. Barla rose and, motioning Aramina to follow her, left his side.

"It is a good dry cave, 'Mina," she said, as if this

were the first chance she had had to inspect it. "There are guards? We must not fail in hospitality."

"Pell remembered to offer, Mother, and they say they have their own rations."

"That is not to the point, 'Mina, and you know it. Would there be more roots in the patch Nexa found yesterday? And nuts, too? For they make a tasty flat bread."

Aramina schooled her features not to betray her dismay, for it took a great many nuts to make a decent quantity of nut flour, and the grinding took hours.

"I'll get nuts, and there may be some wild onions, too," she said, aware of her narrow escape from punishment and determined to be dutiful today.

"Where's Pell? He ought to accompany you."

"He's with K'van, Mother." Aramina picked up her sack, cleaned her belt knife, and sheathed it. She glanced about in the habit of someone used to thinking ahead on chores before she left.

Pell was not with the guards, nor was K'van, although Heth's bronze hide was visible through the trees.

"The boys have gone off to set a wherry snare," the older guard told Aramina with a grin for such youthful pastimes. "There's roosts there." He pointed over the rocky saddle leading to a farther dell.

"A roast wherry would be a real treat for all of us," Aramina said, smiling to include both guards.

"Oh, aye, that it would, young lady." When Aramina started toward the nut plantation, he caught her by the arm. "It's you we're guarding. Where are you going?"

"Only over that ridge"—Aramina pointed to the south—"for nuts."

"I'll just have a look-see." The guard strode along with her, past the sleeping Heth, and up the long slope.

He halted, catching her arm again, as he looked down into the peaceful grove. The nut trees, well grown, were so thick-branched that they had inhibited any undergrowth that the acid of the nut mast had not killed. The approach of humans had sent the wood snakes scurrying, and only the last vestiges of the summer's insects flitted about. Nuts were visible in plenty.

"I'll give you a hand," the guard said, seeing that it was a matter of scooping up the fallen tree fruits.

With two willing pairs of hands, Aramina's sack was filled in short order.

"How much do you need?" the man asked when Aramina began to make a carryall of her jerkin.

"Mother has a mind for nut bread."

The man raised his eyes skyward. "It do be tasty,

and you might just need enough"—he winked broadly at her—"to stuff that wherry your brother plans to snare. I'll just fetch these to your mother. Don't stray now."

Aramina didn't stray, but in gathering she headed toward the far edge of the grove, wondering what other edibles might be found. She filled her jerkin as she moved, and had it stuffed to overflowing when she reached the boundary. There the land fell away into broken boulders. She looked up to the top of the mountain on whose flank she stood. She could see down to a twist of the river rushing through a gorge, just visible through the wintry forest. To be alone, after so many Turns of overcrowding, was a rare treat for Aramina. Maybe Lord Asgenar's gratitude would indeed extend to a longer stay for her family in the cave. It could be made quite tenable, she was sure, even in the coldest weather. Why, they could make stalls for Nudge and Shove, and if Lord Asgenar didn't object, maybe cut steps up the bank. From the fallen trees, they could fashion furniture. Her father could even season wood in the dry rear of the cave and have his own workshop. Her imagination embellished the dazzling possibilities. And then, being a practical girl, she sighed at her folly. She would be content enough to have a secure and private dwelling for as long as it took her father's chest to heal. She mustn't be greedy.

She listened then, as the breeze caressed her face, to what other sounds might be carried up from the river. She wondered if the ambush had been sprung and if she'd hear the sounds of battle. She shivered. Much as she feared Lady Holdless Thella and Giron, she wished only an end to their threat, not their lives.

She heard the faint sound of someone treading close and, thinking it was the guard returning, was taken completely by surprise as a rough hand covered her mouth and strong ones pinned her arms to her sides.

"It falls out well, after all, Giron," said a harsh voice, and Aramina's head was pulled cruelly back by her hair so that she looked up into the stained, sweaty face of Lady Holdless Thella. "We have snared the wild wherry after all, and the trap she laid is bare for Asgenar."

Heth! Heth! Help me! Thella! Even if Giron's heavy hand had not covered her mouth, Aramina was completely paralyzed by fear. Her mind idiotically repeated the one syllable that meant rescue. *Heth! Heth! Heth!*

Giron growled at Aramina as he began to man-handle her across the grove. "Don't struggle, girl, or

I'll knock you senseless. Maybe I ought to, Thella," he added, cocking his big fist in preparation. "If she can hear dragons, they can hear her."

"She's never been near a Weyr!" Thella's reply was contemptuous, but the notion, now Giron had planted it, gave her a moment's pause. Her face con-

torted with anger, she gave Aramina's hair another savage jerk. "Don't even think of calling for a dragon."

Aramina couldn't have stopped her mind's chant, but she frantically rolled her eyes as if complying with Thella's order. Anything to relieve the pain of her scalp.

"Too late!" Giron threw Aramina from him, a heave that left a hunk of her hair and scalp in Thella's hand and Aramina teetering on the brink of a drop. A drop that was blocked by Heth, his eyes whirling red and orange in anger. He bellowed, sinuously weaving in among the trees, chasing Thella and Giron. From the other side of the grove came the two guards, Pell, and K'van, shouting imprecations. Aramina saw Giron and Thella disappear into the woods. The guards ran past in full pelt, but Heth had to stop at the edge of the grove, the forest being too dense for him to penetrate. He continued to bellow in fury, even after K'van reached him.

Shaking with reaction to her frightening experience, Aramina slumped against the nearest bulgenut tree, clasping it for support and trying not to weep so childishly.

" 'Mina! What happened to you?" Pell knelt beside her, his hand hovering over the bleeding scalp wound. "It was really Thella? Who else was with her?"

K'van was beside her, patting her shoulders.

"You did the right thing, 'Mina. Heth heard you and told me. We were setting snares. Heth's called for reinforcements. They won't get away. If there hadn't been so many trees, Heth would've caught 'em already!"

"Dragons," she said in gasps, "aren't built . . . to run in forests." Sniffing, she pointed to Heth, who was retracing his way, weaving in and out of the trees, snarling as one wing caught on a protruding branch. He looked so funny; she oughtn't to laugh at the dear dragon who had saved her from Thella and Giron, but it *was* funny, and she began to giggle and then couldn't stop her laughing.

"What's so funny!" demanded Pell, outraged by his sister's laughter.

"I expect she's a bit hysterical. Not that I blame her. You take her other arm, Pell. We've got to get her back to the cave."

"What about Heth?"

Heth rejoined them, his roars now reduced to belly rumbles.

I told her I was coming! I told her I heard her! Didn't you hear me, 'Mina? Heth curled his neck around K'van to peer anxiously up at Aramina.

Hiccuping somewhere between laughter and tears, Aramina speechlessly patted Heth's muzzle.

I was so scared . . . even her thought hiccuped *. . . I couldn't even hear myself.*

"Shards!" said K'van as a whoosh of wind signaled the arrival of a wing of dragons. Heth swiveled his head toward the display.

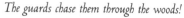

The guards chase them through the woods!

As the three youngsters watched, Aramina marveling at the snippets of conversations she caught in the confusion of orders given and received, the dragons began to peel off from the wing formation, going in all directions in a search for the renegades.

"T'gellan's leading the wing," K'van informed them, deftly picking out of the stream the information that escaped Aramina. "They'll search. We're to get back to the cave."

"Oh, my sackful of nuts!" cried Aramina.

"Nuts, she worries about! At a time like this!" Pell was disgusted.

Aramina started to cry again, unable to stop the tears. "Mother *needs* them for bread flour. . . ."

"I'll come back for 'em," exclaimed Pell at the top of his voice in frustration. "I'll come back!"

Not completely reassured, since she knew her brother so well, Aramina was nonetheless willing to be helped back to the cave. Her mother, after her first startlement, bathed and salved Aramina's scalp and the other scratches she had received from the rough handling. If Barla did so with compressed lips and a decidedly pale face, she did not scold Aramina. Pell, under K'van's stern eye, had gone back for the nuts and Aramina's jerkin. K'van brewed more *klah*, a very welcome cup that infused Aramina's cold stomach with welcome heat.

Aramina, Lessa waits without, said Heth. *For your mother, too.*

"Mother, we're wanted outside," Aramina said.

"By whom?"

"By Lessa, the Weyrwoman of Pern," said K'van. "Heth just relayed the message."

Barla looked at her daughter as if she had never really seen her clearly before.

"You don't just hear dragons," she said in a puzzled voice, "they hear you, and they talk to you, and you can answer them?"

"A very useful knack," K'van said with a grin; then he added, "Lessa's waiting."

"Is she angry with me?" Aramina asked timorously.

"Why would she be angry with you?" K'van asked, puzzled.

We could not be angry with you, Aramina, said the most beautiful dragon voice that Aramina had yet heard.

"C'mon." K'van took Aramina firmly by the arm to haul her out of the cave. "You don't keep Lessa waiting."

Aramina's first impression of the slender figure standing in the clearing was surprise. The Weyrwoman of Benden was so small in stature: a full head shorter than Aramina. But, once Aramina confronted Lessa, the vivid eyes and the forceful personality made her forget about such a trivial detail as height. Nor had Heth mentioned that F'lar and Lord Asgenar also waited.

"My dear child, are you quite all right?" Lessa's expression turned anxious as her hand hovered over the ugly bare patch on Aramina's head.

"I don't know how that villian Thella eluded us," said Asgenar, his teeth clenched with frustration. "We have captured the rest of her band. Fewer to trouble you, and us. I am most chagrined, Aramina, that despite our precautions you were put at risk."

"I'm fine, really, Lord Asgenar. Heth saved me. And Mother had the fellis and numbweed."

"We are extremely grateful to you," Barla put in, "for those generous gifts."

"Generous!" Lessa made a scathing remark. "I would be a lot more generous, Lady Barla, if your stiff Ruathan pride would permit."

Nothing could have startled Barla more, but, though she permitted a slight smile to curve her lips, to Aramina she seemed to be more prideful than ever.

"We Ruathans have reason to be proud, Lady Lessa."

"But not stupid in that pride, Lady Barla. Lytol tells me that Dowell's hold is still vacant. Deserted, needing repairs, for no one under Fax's holding prospered. Would you prefer to return there? Lord Asgenar"—Asgenar bowed at his name—"is also interested in anyone with wood mastery."

Barla looked from one to the other. "Ruatha is ours by right."

"So be it, Lady Barla," Lessa said, and, from the way her mouth twitched, Aramina was certain that she applauded the answer.

"However, Lord Asgenar, I am certain that my husband would be glad to build you a Gather wagon . . . to acquit our lodging here."

"Only if he also accepts the marks his Craft allots for the labor," said Asgenar with a wide grin.

"Of course, Aramina is for Benden Weyr," Lessa went on, her eyes now fixed on Barla's face.

"But I want to go home, to Ruatha!" cried Aramina, clinging to her mother now; clinging, too, to the dream on which she had been nourished from childhood, the return to the place of her birth, where her family belonged.

"A girl who hears dragons belongs to the Weyr," said Barla, firmly taking Aramina's hands and pressing them hard.

"It's not as if you can't visit any time you want to," Lessa said lightly. "I do. Though we of Ruatha serve our Weyrs whenever we are called to."

Please, 'Mina. Heth's tremulous whisper invaded her conflicting thoughts. *Please come to Benden with me and K'van. We'd love to have you.*

You will be most welcome in Benden Weyr, said the dark, black, rich voice of Mnementh.

"There are eggs hardening on Benden Hatching Ground right now," Lessa went on, her voice persuasive. "Benden needs a girl who can hear dragons."

"More than my family needs me?" asked Aramina perversely.

"Far more, as you'll discover," said Lessa, holding her hand out to Aramina. "Coming?"

"I don't have a choice, do I?" But Aramina smiled.

"Not when Lessa, and Benden's dragons, have made up your mind for you," said F'lar with a laugh.

From the track, dragons bellowed an emphatic agreement.

RUNNER
OF
PERN

*T*enna topped the rise and paused to catch her breath, leaning forward, hands on her knees to ease her back muscles. Then, as she had been taught, she walked along the top on what flat space there was, kicking out her legs and shaking the thigh muscles, breathing through her mouth until she stopped panting. Taking her water bottle from her belt, she allowed herself a swig, swishing it around in her mouth to moisturize the dry tissue. She spat out that mouthful and took another, letting this one slowly trickle down her throat. The night was cool enough to keep her from sweating too heavily. But she wouldn't be standing around long enough to get a chill.

It didn't take long for her breath to return to normal, and she was pleased by that. She was in good shape. She kicked out her legs to ease the strain she had put on them to make the height. Then, settling her belt and checking the message pouch, she started down the hill at a rapid walking pace. It was too dark—Belior had not yet risen above the plain to give her full light for the down side of the hill—to be safe to run in shadows. She only knew this part of the trace by word of mouth, not actually footing it. She'd done well so far during this, her second Turn of running, and had made most of her first Cross by the suggested easy laps. Runners watched out for one another, and no station manager would overtax a novice. With any luck, she'd've made it all the way to the Western Sea in the next sevenday. This was the first big test of her apprenticeship as an express runner. And really she'd only the Western Range left to cross once she got to Fort Hold.

Halfway down from the top of the rise, she met the ridge crest she'd been told about and, with the usual check of the pouch she carried, she picked up her knees and started the ground-eating lope that was the pride of a Pernese runner.

Of course, the legendary "lopers"—the ones who had been able to do a hundred miles in a day— had perished ages ago, but their memory was kept alive. Their endurance and dedication were an example to everyone who ran the traces of Pern. There hadn't been many of them, according to the legend, but they had started the runner stations when the need for the rapid delivery of messages arose, during the First Fall of Thread. Lopers had been able to put themselves in some sort of trance which not only allowed them to run extended distances but kept them warm during snowstorms and in freezing temperatures. They had also planted the original traces, which now were a network crisscrossing the entire continent.

While only Lord Holders and Craftmasters could afford to keep runnerbeasts for their couriers, the average person, wanting to contact crafthalls, relatives, or friends across Pern, could easily afford to express a letter across the continent in runner pouches, carried from station to station. Others might call them "holds," but runners had always had "stations," and station agents, as part of *their* craft history. Drum messages were great for short messages, if the weather was right and the winds didn't interrupt the beat, but as long as folks wanted to send written messages there'd be runners to take them.

Tenna often thought proudly of the tradition she was carrying on. It was a comfort on long solitary journeys. Right now, the running was good: the ground was firm but springy, a surface that had been assiduously maintained since the ancient runners had planted it. Not only did the mossy stuff make running easier but it identified a runner's path. A runner would instantly feel the difference in the surface, if he, or she, strayed off the trace.

Slowly, as full Belior rose behind her, her way became illuminated by the moon's light and she picked up her pace, running easily, breathing freely, her hands carried high, chest height, with elbows tucked in. No need to leave a "handle," as her father called it, to catch the wind and slow the pace. At times like these, with good footing, a fair light, and a cool evening, you felt like you could run forever. If there weren't a sea to stop you.

She ran on, able to see the flow of the ridge, and by the time the trace started to descend again, Belior was high enough to light her way. She saw the stream ahead and slowed cautiously . . . though she'd been told that the ford had a good pebbly surface . . . and splashed through the ankle-high cold water, up onto the bank, veering slightly south, picking up the trace again by its springy surface.

She'd be over halfway now to Fort Hold and should make it by dawn. This was a well-traveled route, southwest along the coast to the farther Holds. Most of what she carried right now was destined for Fort Holders, so it was the end of the line for both the pouch and herself. She'd heard so much about the facilities at Fort that she didn't quite believe it. Runners tended to understatement rather than exaggeration. If a runner told you a trace was dangerous, you believed it! But what they said about Fort was truly amazing.

Tenna came from a running family: father, uncles, cousins, grandfathers, brothers, sisters, and two aunts were all out and about the traces that crisscrossed Pern from Nerat Tip to High Reaches Hook, from Benden to Boll.

"It's bred in us," her mother had said, answering the queries of her younger children. Cesila managed a large runner station, just at the northern Lemos end of the Keroon plains where the immense skybroom trees began. Strange trees that flourished only in that region of Pern. Trees that, a much younger Tenna had been sure, were where the Benden Weyr dragons took a rest in their flights across the continent. Cesila had laughed at Tenna's notion.

"The dragons of Pern don't need to rest anywhere, dear. They just go *between* to wherever they need to go. You probably saw some of them out hunting their weekly meal."

In her running days, Cesila had completed nine full Crosses a Turn until she'd married another runner and started producing her own bag of runners-to-be.

"Lean we are in the breeding, and leggy, most of us, with big lungs and strong bones. Ah, there now, a few come out who're more for speed than distance but they're handy enough at Gathers, passing the winning line before the others have left the starting ribbon. We have our place on the world same as holders and even weyrfolk. Each to his, or her, own. Weaver and tanner, and farmer, and fisher, and smith and runner and all."

"That's not the way we was taught to sing the Duty Song," Tenna's younger brother had remarked.

"Maybe," Cesila had said with a grin, "but it's the way I sing it and you can, too. I must have a word with the next harper through here. He can change his words if he wants us to take his messages." And she gave her head one of her emphatic shakes to end that conversation.

As soon as runner-bred children reached full growth, they were tested to see if they'd the right Blood for the job. Tenna's legs had stopped growing by the time she'd reached her fifteenth full Turn. That was when she was assessed by a senior runner of another Bloodline. Tenna had been very nervous, but her mother, in her usual offhanded way, had given her lanky daughter a long knowing look.

"Nine children I've given your father, Fedri, and

four are already runners. You'll be one, too, never fear."

"But Sedra's . . ."

Cesila held up her hand. "I know your sister's mated and breeding but she did two Crosses before she found a man she had to have. So she counts, too. Gotta have proper Bloodlines to breed proper runners and it's us who do that." Cesila paused to be sure Tenna would not interrupt again. "I came from a hold with twelve, all of them runners. And all breeding runners. You'll run, girl. Put your mind at ease. You'll run." Then she'd laughed. "It's for how long, not will you, for a female."

Tenna had decided a long time ago—when she had first been considered old enough to mind her younger siblings—that she'd prefer running to raising runners. She'd run until she could no longer lift her knees. She'd an aunt who'd never mated: ran until she was older than Cesila was now and then took over the management of a connecting station down Igen way. Should something happen and she couldn't run anymore, Tenna wouldn't mind managing a station. Her mother ran hers proper, always had hot water ready to ease a runner's aching limbs, good food, comfortable beds, and healing skills that rivaled what you could find in any Hold. And it was always exciting, for you never knew who might run in that day, or where they'd be going. Runners crossed the continent regularly, bringing with them news from other parts of Pern. Many had interesting tales to tell of problems on the trace and how to cope with them. You heard all about other Holds and Halls, and the one dragonweyr, as well as what interested runners most specifically: what conditions were like and where traces might need maintenance after a heavy rain or landslide.

She was mightily relieved, however, when her father said he had asked Mallum of the Telgar station to do her assessment. At least Tenna had met the man on those occasions when he'd been through to their place on the edge of Keroon's plains. Like other runners, he was a lanky length of man, with a long face and graying hair that he tied back with his sweatband as most runners did.

Her parents didn't tell her when Mallum was expected, but he turned up one bright morning, handing in a pouch to be logged on the board by the door and then limping to the nearest seat.

"Bruised the heel. We'll have to rock that south trace again. I swear it grows new ones every Turn or two," he said, mopping his forehead with his orange sweatband and thanking Tenna for the cup of water.

"Cesila, got some of that sheer magic poultice of yours?"

"I do. Put the kettle to heat the moment I saw you struggling up the trace."

"Was not struggling," Mallum said in jovial denial. "Was careful not to put the heel down was all."

"Don't try to fool me, you spavined gimper," Cesila replied as she was dipping a poultice sack into the heated water, testing it with a finger.

"Who's to run on? Some orders in that need to be got south smartly."

"I'm taking it on," Fedri said, coming out of his room and tying on his sweatband. "How urgent?" His runner's belt was draped over his shoulder. "I've others to add from the morning's eastern run."

"Hmmm. They want to make the Igen Gather."

"Ha! It'll be there betimes," Fedri said, reaching for the pouch and carefully adding the other messages to it before he put it through the belt loops. Settling it in the small of his back with one hand, he chalked up the exchange time with the other. "See you."

Then he was out the door and turning south, settling into his long-distance stride almost as soon as his foot hit the moss of the trace.

Tenna, knowing what was needed, had already

pulled a footstool over to Mallum. She looked up at him for permission and, with his nod, unlaced the right shoe, feeling the fine quality of the leather. Mallum made his own footwear and he had set the stitching fine and tight.

Cesila knelt beside her daughter, craning her head to see the bruise.

"Hmmm. Hit it early on, didn'tcha?"

"I did," Mallum said, drawing his breath in with a hiss as Cesila slapped the poultice on. "Oooooh! Shards . . . you didn't get it too hot, didja?"

Cesila sniffed denial in reply as she neatly and deftly tied the packet to his foot.

"And is this the lass of yours as is to be taken for a run?" he asked, relaxing his expression from the grimace he'd made when the poultice was first applied. "Prettiest of the bunch." And he grinned at Tenna.

"Handsome is as handsome does," Cesila said. "Looks is all right but long legs is better. Tenna's her name."

"Handsome's not a bad thing to be, Cesila, and it's obvious your daughter takes after you."

Cesila sniffed again but Tenna could see that her mother didn't mind Mallum's remarks. And Cesila was a handsome woman: lithe still and slender, with graceful hands and feet. Tenna wished she were more like her mother.

"Nice long line of leg," Mallum went on approvingly. He beckoned for Tenna to come closer and had a good look at the lean muscles, then asked to see her bare feet. Runners tended to walk barefooted a lot. Some even ran barefooted. "Good bone. Hmmm. Nice lean frame. Hmm. Not a pick on you, girl. Hope you can keep warm enough in winter like that." That was such an old runner comment, but his jollity was encouraging and Tenna was ever so glad that Mallum was her assessor. He was always pleasant on his short stops at Station 97. "We'll take a short one tomorrow when this foot's eased."

More runners came in so Cesila and Tenna were busy, checking in messages, sorting the packets for the changeovers, serving food, heating water for baths, tending scratched legs. It was spring of the year and most runners only used leggings during the coldest months.

Enough stayed the night so there was good chatter and gossip to entertain. And prevent Tenna from worrying about satisfying her assessor on the morning.

A runner had come in late that night, on her way

north, with some messages to be transferred to an eastern route. His heel bruise much eased, Mallum thought he could take those on.

"It's a good testing trot," he said, and gestured for Tenna to slip the message pouch on her belt. "I'll travel light, girl." His grin was teasing, for the pouch weighed little more than the wherhide it was made from. "First, lemme see what you wear on your feet."

She showed him her shoes, the most important part of a runner's gear. She'd used her family's special oils to soften the wherhide and then formed it on the lasts that had been carved for her feet by her uncle who did them for her Bloodline. Her stitches were neat but not as fine as Mallum's. She intended to improve. Meanwhile, this pair wasn't a bad effort and fit her feet like gloves. The spikes were medium length as fit for the present dry trace conditions. Most long-distance runners carried an extra pair with shorter spikes for harder ground, especially during spring and summer. She was working on her winter footwear, hoping she'd need it, for those boots came up to midcalf and required a lot more conditioning. Even they were of lighter weight than the footgear holders would use. But then most holders plodded and the thicker leather was suitable for their tasks as fine soft hide was right for a runner's foot.

Mallum nodded in approval as he handed back her shoes. Now he checked the fit of her belt to be sure it was snug enough not to rub against the small of her back as she ran, and made certain that her short trunks would not pull against her leg and that her sleeveless top covered her backside well below her waist to help prevent her getting a kidney chill. Stopping often from a need to relieve oneself ruined the rhythm of a run.

"We'll go now," Mallum said, having assured himself that she was properly accoutred.

Cesila stood in the door, gave her daughter a reassuring nod, and saw them off, up the eastern trace. Before they were out of sight, she gave the particular runner yodel that stopped them in their tracks. They saw her pointing skyward: at the arrow formation of dragons in the sky, a most unusual sight these days when the dragons of Benden Weyr were so rarely seen.

To see dragons in the sky was the best sort of omen. They were there . . . and then they weren't! She smiled. Too bad runners couldn't just *think* themselves to their destinations the way dragons could. As if he had shared her thought, Mallum grinned back at her and then turned to face the direction in which they were headed, and any nervousness Tenna

had had disappeared. When he sprang off again, she was in step with him by the third stride. He nodded again approvingly.

"Running's not just picking up your heels and showing them to those behind you," Mallum said, his eyes watching the trace ahead, though he must have known it as well as Tenna did. "A good bit of proper running is learning to pace yourself and your stride. It's knowing the surfaces of the traces you have to traverse. It's knowing how to save your strength so you'll last the longer hauls. When to ease back to a walk, when and how to drink and eat so's you're not too gutty to run right. It's learning the routes of the various Crosses and what sort of weather you might have to run through . . . and learning to maneuver on snowrunners on the northern Crosses. And, most important, when to take cover and just let the weather have its way with the world and you safe out of it. So's the messages and the packets you carry will get through as soon as possible."

She had responded with a nod of appreciation. Not that she hadn't heard the same lecture time and again in the station from every relative and runner. But this time it was for her benefit and she owed Mallum the courtesy of listening closely. She did watch Mallum's stride, though, to be sure his heel wasn't bothering him. He caught her glance once and gave her a grin.

"Be sure you carry a wedge of that poultice on any long laps, girl. You never know, you know, when you might need it. As I just did." And he grimaced, reminding Tenna that even the best runner can put a foot wrong.

While no runner carries much, the long-tailed orange sweatband that runners invariably wore could be used to strap a strain or sprain. An oiled packet, no larger than the palm of a hand, had a cloth soaked in numbweed which both cleansed and eased the scratches one could acquire from time to time. Simple remedies for the most common problems. A wedge of poultice could be added to such travel gear and be well worth its weight.

Tenna had no trouble making that lap with Mallum even when he picked up the pace on the flat section.

"Running with a pretty girl's not hard to do," he told her when they took one brief pause.

She wished he didn't make so much of her looks. They wouldn't help her run any better or help her become what she wanted to be: a top runner.

By the time they reached Irma's station at midday, she was not even breathing very hard. But the moment Mallum slowed, he limped slightly with his full weight on the heel.

"Hmm. Well, I can wait out the day here with more poultice," he said, pulling the little wedge from one of the pockets of his belt. "See," and he displayed it to Tenna, "handy enough."

She tapped her aid pocket and smiled.

Old Irma came out with a grin on her sun-dried face for them.

"Will she do, Mallum?" the old woman asked, handing each a cup.

"Oh, aye, she'll do. A credit to her Bloodline and not a bother to run with!" Mallum said with a twinkle in his eyes.

"I pass, do I, Mallum?" Tenna asked, needing to have a direct answer.

"Oh, aye," and he laughed, walking about and shaking his legs to get the kinks out even as she was doing. "No fear on that. Any hot water for m'poultice, Irm?"

"Coming up." She ducked back into her station and came out with a bowl of steaming water which

she set down on the long bench that was an in-
evitable fixture of every station. The overhang of the
roof provided a shelter from sun and rain. Most
runners were obsessed with watching the traces to
see who was coming and going. The long bench, its
surface smoothed by generations of bums sliding
across it, was placed so that it commanded a good
view of the four traces linking at Irma's.

Automatically, Tenna pulled a footstool from
under the bench and held out her hand to receive
Mallum's right foot. She untied the shoe, and placed
the now moistened poultice on the bruise while
Irma handed her a bandage to fix it in place, taking
a good look at the injury in the process.

" 'Nother day'll do it. Shoulda stayed off it this
mornin', too."

"Not when I'd a chance to run with such a pretty
girl," Mallum said.

"Just like a man," Irma said dismissively.

Tenna felt herself blushing, although she was beginning to believe he wasn't just teasing. No one else
had ever commented on her looks.

"It wasn't a taxing leg, Irma. It's level most of
the way and a good surface," she said, grinning
shyly at Mallum as she tried to divert Irma's criti-
cism.

"Humph! Well, a hill run would've been down-right foolish and it is flat this way."

"Anything for Tenna to take back," Mallum asked, getting back to business, "to make her first round-trip as a runner?"

"Should be," Irma said, winking at Tenna for this informal inclusion into the ranks of Pern runners. "You could eat now . . . soup's ready and so's the bread."

"Wouldn't mind a bit myself," Mallum said, carefully shifting his position as if easing the heat from the poultice, since the heat probably penetrated even the toughened sole of his foot.

By the time Tenna had eaten the light meal, two runners came in: a man she didn't know by sight, on a long leg from Bitra with a pouch to go farther west; and one of Irma's sons.

"I can run it to Ninety-Seven," she said, the official designation of her family's station.

"That'll do," the man said, panting and heaving from his long haul. "That'll do fine." He gasped for more breath. "It's an urgent," he got out. "Your name?"

"Tenna."

"One . . . of . . . Fedri's?" he asked and she nod-ded. "That's good . . . enough for me. Ready to . . . hit the trace?"

"Sure." She held out her hand for the pouch that he slipped off his belt, pausing only to mark the pass-over time on the flap as he gave it into her keeping. "You are?" she asked, sliding the pouch onto her own belt and settling it in the small of her back.

"Masso," he said, reaching now for the cup of water Irma had hastened to bring him. He whooshed her off to the westward trace. With a final grateful farewell wave to Mallum, she picked up her heels as Mallum cheered her on with the traditional runner's "yo-ho."

She made it home in less time than it had taken her to reach Irma's, and one of her brothers was there to take the pouch on the next westward lap. Silan nodded approval at the pass-over time, marked his own receipt, and was off.

"So, girl, you're official," her mother said, and embraced her. "And no need to sweat it at all, was there?"

"Running's not always as easy," her father said from the bench, "but you made good time and that's a grand way to start. I hadn't expected you back before midafternoon."

Tenna did the short legs all around Station 97 for the first summer and into that winter, building her stamina for longer runs and becoming known at all the connecting stations. She made her longest run to Greystones, on the coast, just ahead of a very bad snowstorm. Then, because she was the only runner available in Station 18 when the exhausted carrier of an urgent message came in, she had to carry it two stations north. A fishing sloop would be delayed back to port until a new mast could be stepped. Since the vessel was overdue, there were those who'd be very glad to get the message she carried.

Such emergency news should have been drummed ahead, but the high winds would tear such a message to nonsense. It was a tough run, with cold as well as wind and snow across a good bit of the low-lying trace. Pacing herself, she did take an hour's rest in one of the Thread shelters that dotted a trace. She made the distance in such good time in those conditions that she got extra stitches on her belt, marking her rise toward journeyman rank.

This run to Fort Hold would be two more stitches on her belt if she finished in good time. And she was sure she would... with the comforting sort of certainty that older runners said you began to sense when you'd been traveling the traces awhile. She was also now accustomed to judging how long she had run by the feeling in her legs. There was none of the leaden feeling that accompanied real fatigue, and she was still running easily. So long as she had no leg cramp, she knew she could continue effortlessly at this good pace until she reached Station 300 at Fort. Leg cramp was always a hazard and could strike you without warning. She was careful to renew the tablets a runner chewed to ease off a cramp. And was not too slow about grabbing a handful of any useful herbs she spotted which would help prevent the trouble.

She oughtn't to be letting her mind wander like this, but with an easy stride and a pleasant night in which to travel, it was hard to keep her mind on the job. She would, smartly enough, if there were complications like bad weather or poor light. This was also far too well traveled country for there to be dangers like tunnel snakes, which were about the worst risk that runners encountered—usually at dawn or dusk, when the creatures were out hunting. Of course, renegades, while not as common as tunnel snakes, were more dangerous, since they were human, not animal, but that distinction was often moot. As runners rarely carried marks, they were not as likely to be waylaid as were messengers on runnerbeasts, or other solitary travelers. Tenna hadn't heard of any renegade attacks this far west, but sometimes those people were so vicious that they might pull up a runner just for spite and malice. In the past three Turns, there had been two cases—and those up in northern Lemos and Bitra—where runners had been hamstrung out of sheer malevolence.

Once in a while, in a bad winter, a flock of very hungry wherries might attack a runner in the open, but the instances were rare enough. Snakes were the most likely danger encountered, particularly midsummer, when there were newly hatched clutches.

Her father had had injuries two summers back with such a hazard. He'd been amazed at how fast the adult tunnel snake could move when alarmed. Mostly they were torpid creatures, only hunger quickening them. But he'd stepped in the midst of an ill-placed nest and had had the hatchlings swarming up his legs, pricking the skin in innumerable places and even managing to get as high as his crotch. (Her mother had stifled a giggle and remarked that it had been more than her father's pride that had been wounded.) But he'd scars from claw and tooth that he could show.

Moonlit nights like this one were a joy to run in, with the air cool enough to dry the sweat on her face and chest, the trace springy underfoot and clear ahead of her. And her thoughts could wander.

There would be a Gather shortly after she reached her destination; she knew she was carrying some orders for Crafts displaying at Fort Hold. Pouches were invariably fuller going to or coming from a Gather—orders from those unable to attend, wishing to contact a Mastercraftsman. Maybe, if she was lucky, she could stay over for the Gather. She hadn't been to one in a long while and she did want to find well-tanned leathers for a new pair of running shoes. She'd enough money to her credit to give a fair price for the right hides: she'd checked the books her mother kept of her laps. Most Halls were quite willing to take a runner-station chit. She'd one in a belt pocket. If she found just the right skins, she'd a bit of leeway to bargain, above and beyond the surface value of the chit.

A Gather would be fun, too. She loved dancing, and was very good at the toss dance, if she could find someone who could properly partner her in it. Fort was a good Hold. And the music would be special, seeing as how the Harper Hall was right there in Fort.

She ran on, tunes of harper melodies flitting

through her mind even if she'd no breath to sing them.

She was running along a long curve now, around an upthrust of rock—most traces were as straight as possible—and brought her mind back to her directions. Just around this curve, she should find a trace turning off to the right, inland, toward Fort. She must pay attention now so she wouldn't have to break stride and backtrack.

Suddenly she could feel vibrations through her feet, though she could see nothing around the vegetation banking the curve. Listening intently, she could now hear an odd *phuff-phuff* sound, coming closer, getting louder. The sound was just enough of a warning for her to move left, out of the center of the trace, where she'd have just that much more of a glimpse of what was making the sound and the vibrations. This was a runner track, not a trail or road. No runner made those sounds, or hit the ground that hard to make vibrations. She saw the dark mass bearing down on her, and flung herself into the undergrowth as runnerbeast and rider came within a finger span of knocking into her. She could feel the wind of their passing and smell the sweat of the beast.

"Stupid!" she shouted after them, getting branches

and leaves in her mouth as she fell, feeling needly gouges in the hands she had put out to break her fall. She spent the next minute struggling to her feet and spitting bitter leaves and twigs out of her mouth. They left behind an acrid, drying taste: sticklebush! She'd fallen into a patch of sticklebush.

At this time of the Turn, there were no leaves yet to hide the hairlike thorns that coated twig and branch. A nuisance which balanced out their gift of succulent berries in the autumn.

Nor did the rider falter, or even pull up, when the least he could have done was return to be sure

she hadn't been injured. Surely he'd seen her? Surely he'd heard her outraged shout. And what was *he* doing, using a runner trace in the first place? There was a good road north for ordinary travelers.

"I'll get you!" she called, shaking her fist with frustration.

She was shaking with reaction to such a near miss. Then she became uncomfortably aware of the scratches on hands, arms, legs, chest, and two on one cheek. Stamping with fury, she got the numbweed from her belt pocket and daubed at the cuts, hissing as the solution stung. But she didn't want the sap to get into her blood. Nor did she want the slivers to work in. She managed to pick the ones out of her hands, daubing the numbweed into those. She couldn't really see the extent of her injuries, some being down the back of her arm. She picked out what slivers she could and carefully pressed in the pad until all the moisture was gone from it. Even if she had avoided infection, she was likely to be teased about falling when she got to the station. Runners were supposed to keep *on* their feet, and in balance. Not that a rider had any business on the trace. Surely that would also help her find out who the rider had been, besides being bold enough to ride a runner trace. And if she wasn't around to give him a fat lip, maybe another runner would give the lesson in her place. Runners were not above complaining to Lord Holders or their stewards if someone abused their rights.

Having done as much as she could then, she stifled her anger: that didn't get the pouch to its destination. And she mustn't let her anger get the better of common sense. The brush with disaster, close as it was, had resulted in very minor problems, she told herself firmly. What were scratches! But she found it hard to regain her stride. She'd been going so smoothly, too, and so close to the end of this lap.

She could have been killed, smacking into a runnerbeast at the speeds they'd both been traveling. If she hadn't thought to move out of the center of the trace . . . where she had every right to be, not him . . . if she hadn't felt the hoofbeats through her shoes and heard the animal's high breathing . . . Why, both sets of messages could have been delayed! Or lost.

Her legs felt tired and heavy and she had to concentrate hard to try to regain the rhythm. Reluctantly she realized that she was unlikely to and settled for conserving her energy.

Running into the end of night, the dawn behind her, was not as much a pleasure as it could have been, and that annoyed Tenna even more. Just wait till she found out who that rider was! She'd tell him a thing or two. Though common sense told her that she was unlikely to encounter him. He was outbound and she was inbound. If he'd been in that much of a hurry, he might be a relay rider, bound for a distant location. Lord Holders could afford such services and the stabling of fast runnerbeasts along the way. But he shouldn't have been on a runner trace. There were roads for beasts! Hooves could tear up the surface of the trace and the station manager might have to spend hours replacing divots torn up by shod hooves. Traces were for runners. She kept returning to that indignant thought. She just hoped any other runner on the trace would hear him in time! *That's one reason you keep your mind on your run, Tenna.* Even if you'd no reason to suspect you weren't alone with the night and the moon on a runner trace.

The runner station was just below the main entrance to Fort Hold. History had it that Fort had started runners as short-distance messengers, hundreds and hundreds of Turns ago, even before drum towers were built. Fort Hold had utilized the skills of runners for many tasks, especially during Threadfall, when runners had accompanied all ground crews, vital as couriers in emergencies. The installation of the drum towers and the development of runnerbeasts had not put an end to the need for the runners of Pern. This main connecting hold was the largest ever built just to house and care for runners. Three levels high, she'd been told, and several back into the Fort cliff. It also boasted one of the best bathing facilities on the continent: hot running water in deep tubs that had eased centuries of runner aches and pains. Cesila had highly recommended that Tenna try for Fort when she got that far west. And here she was and right ready to appreciate the accommodations.

She was very weary and not only out of pace but jarring herself with every step down the broader avenue that led to her destination. Her hands stung from the sap and she hoped she hadn't any slivers left in them. But hands were a long way from the feet.

Beastholders, up early to feed stock, gave her cheery waves and smiles, and their courtesies somewhat restored her good humor. She did not care to arrive petulant as well as scratched, not on her first visit here.

Almost as if the manager had a special sensitivity to incoming runners, the double door was thrown open as she came to a rough, gasping halt, hand raised to catch the bell cord.

"Thought I heard someone coming." The man, a welcoming grin on his face, put out both hands to steady her. He was one of the oldest men she had ever seen: his skin was a network of wrinkles and grooves, but his eyes were bright—for this hour—and he looked to be a merry man. "New one, too, at that, for all you look familiar to me. A pretty face is a great sight on a fine morning."

Sucking in breath enough to give her name, Tenna paced into the large entry room. She unbuckled her message pouch as she eased the tension in her leg muscles.

"Tenna passing Two-Oh-Eight with eastern messages. Fort's the destination for all."

"Welcome to Three Hundred, Tenna," he said, taking the pouch from her and immediately chalking up her arrival on the heavy old board to the left of the station door. "All for here, huh?" He passed her a cup before he opened the pouch, to check the recipients.

With cup in hand, she went out again, still flicking her legs to ease the muscles. First she rinsed her mouth, spitting out that first mouthful onto the cobbles. Then she would sip to swallow. Nor was this just water but some sort of fresh-tasting drink that refreshed dry tissues.

"You're a mite the worse for the run," the man said, standing in the door and pointing to the bloody smears on her bare skin. "What'd you run into?"

"Sticklebush," she said through gritted teeth. "Runnerbeast ran me off 'round the hill curve ... galloping along a *runner* trace like he must know he shouldn't." She was astonished at the anger in her voice when she'd meant to sound matter-of-fact.

"That'd be Haligon, more'n likely," the station keeper said, nodding with a disapproving scowl. "Saw him peltin' down to the beasthold an hour or so ago. I've warned him myself about using the traces but he says it cuts half an hour off a trip and he's conducting an ex-per-i-ment."

"He might have killed me," she said, her anger thoroughly fanned.

"You'd better tell him. Maybe a pretty runner'll get it through his thick skull because the odd crack or two hasn't."

His reaction made Tenna feel that her anger was righteous. It's one thing to be angry on your own, another to have confirmation of your right to be angry. She felt redeemed. Though she couldn't see why being pretty would be an advantage if you were giving someone what-for. She could hit just as hard as the ugliest runner she'd ever met.

"You'll need a long soak with sticklebush slivers in you. You did have something to put on 'em right then, didn't you?" When she nodded, now annoyed because he implied that she might not have that much sense, he added, "I'll can send m'mate to look at those cuts. Wrong time of the Turn to fall into sticklebush, ya know." And she nodded her head vigorously. "All in all, you made a good time from Two-Oh-Eight," he added, approvingly. "Like that in a young runner. Shows you're not just a pretty face. Now, go up the stairs there, take your first right, go along the corridor, fourth door on the left. No one else's up. Towels on the shelves. Leave your clothes: they'll be washed and dry by evening. You'll want a good feed after a night run and then a good long sleep. We've all for you, runner."

She thanked him, turned to the stairs, and then tried to lift the wooden blocks her legs had become up the steps. Her toes dragged as she made her feet move, and she was grateful for the carpeting that saved the wooden stairs from her spikes. But then this place was for runners, shoes, spikes, and all.

"Fourth door," she murmured to herself, and pushed against a portal that opened into the most spacious bathing room she'd ever seen. And pungent with something pleasantly astringent. Nothing as grand as this even at Keroon Hold. Five tubs ranged along the back wall with curtains to separate them if one needed privacy. There were two massage tables, sturdy, padded, with shelves of oils and salves underneath. They would account for the nice smells. The room was hot and she began to sweat again, a sweat that made her nicks and scratches itch. There were changing cubicles, too, to the right of the door . . . and behind her she found oversized towels in stacks higher than her head, and she wasn't short. There were cubbies holding runner pants and shirts for all weathers and the thick anklets that cushioned and warmed weary feet. She took a towel, her fingers feeling the thick, soft nap. It was as big as a blanket.

In the cubicle nearest the tubs, she shucked off her garments, automatically folding them into a neat pile. Then, looping the towel over the hook set by the side of the tub for that purpose, she eased herself into the warm water. The tub was taller than she was and she let herself down to touch a floor, a full hand of water above her head when she did. Amazing!

This was sheer luxury. She wondered how often

she could draw a run to Fort Hold. The water made her scratches sting, but that was nothing to the comfort it was giving her tired muscles. Swishing around in the large square tub, her hand connected with a ledge, sort of curved, a few inches below the surface. With a grin she realized that she could rest her head on it and be able to float safely. Which was exactly what she did, arms out to her sides, legs dangling. She hadn't known bathing could be so . . . so splendid. She let every muscle in her body go limp. And lay suspended in the water.

"Tenna?" a woman's voice called gently, as if not to startle the lone bather. "I'm Penda, Torlo's mate. He sent me up. I've some herbs for the bath that'll help those scratches. Wrong time of the Turn to fall into sticklebush."

"I know," Tenna agreed dourly. "Be glad of any help." Tenna didn't really want to open her eyes or move but she politely swished herself across the water to the edge of the tub.

"Lemme see them cuts so's I can see didja get any punctures like. That'd be no good with the sap rising," Penda said. She walked quickly to the tub with an odd sideways gait, so whatever had injured her hip had happened a long time ago and she had learned to cope with it. She grinned at Tenna.

"Pretty runner girl, you are. You give Haligon what-for next time you see him."

"How'll I know him?" Tenna asked acerbically, though she dearly wished a confrontation with the rider. "And why is 'pretty' a help?"

"Haligon likes pretty girls." Penda gave an exaggerated wink. "We'll see you stay about long enough to give him what-for. *You* might do some good."

Tenna laughed and, at Penda's gesture, held out her hands and turned her left arm where Penda could see it.

"Hmmm. Mostly surface but there's punctures on the heels of both hands." She ran oddly soft fingers across Tenna's hands, catching on three slivers so that Tenna shivered with the unpleasant sensation. "Soaking'll do the most good. Loosen them up in your skin. Prolly clean 'em all out. Stickle's a clever bush, harming you so, but this'll help," she said, and took a collection of bottles from the deep pocket in her apron and selected one. "Got to leave nothing to chance, ya know," she added as she deftly splashed about twenty drops into the tub water. "Don't worry about emptying the tub, either. It'll run clear and'll be fresh water by the time someone else climbs in. I'll take out the slivers when you've soaked. You want a rub then? Or would you rather sleep first?"

"A bit of a rub would be marvelous, thanks. And before I sleep."

"I'll be back with some food."

Tenna thought of the bathing room in her parents' station and grinned. Nothing to compare to this, though she'd always thought her station was lucky to have a tub so long you could lie out flat in it: even the tallest runners could. But you had to keep the fire going under the tank all the time to be sure there was enough for when a bath was needed. Not like this—the water already hot and you only needing to step into the tub. The herbs scented the steamy water, making it feel softer against her skin. She lay back again.

She was nearly asleep when Penda returned with a tray containing klah, fresh-baked bread, a little pot of, appropriately enough, stickleberry preserve, and a bowl of porridge.

"Messages've already been handed over to them they was sent to, so you can sleep good, knowing the run's well ended."

Tenna consumed her meal, down to the last scrap. Penda was making quite a mixture with the massage oils, and the runner inhaled the scent of them. Then Tenna climbed on the table, letting her body go limp while Penda used a tweezer on the slivers still caught in her flesh. Penda counted as she deposited the wicked hairs. Nine, all told. She applied more medication and the last of the itching and discomfort vanished. Tenna sighed. Then Penda soothed tired muscles and tendons. Her touch was sure but gentle. She did announce that there were more punctures on the backs of Tenna's arms and legs and proceeded to go at them with the tweezers to remove the slivers. That done, her motions became more soothing and Tenna relaxed again.

"There y'are. Just go along to the third door down on your left, Tenna," Penda said softly when she had finished.

Tenna roused enough from the delightful, massage-induced stupor and wrapped the big towel tightly around her chest. Like most runner females, she didn't have much of a bust, but that was an advantage.

"Don't forget these," Penda said, shoving the laces of her running shoes at her. "Clothes'll be clean and dry when you wake."

"Thanks, Penda," Tenna said sincerely, astonished that she'd been drowsy enough to forget her precious shoes.

She padded down the hall in the thick anklets that Penda had slipped on her feet and pushed in the third door. Light from the corridor showed her where the bed was, straight across the narrow space, against the wall. Closing the door, she made her way to it in the dark. Dropping the towel, she leaned down to feel for the edge of the quilt she'd seen folded on the foot of the bed. She pulled it over her as she stretched out. Sighed once and fell asleep.

Good-natured laughter and movement down the hall roused her. Someone had half opened the glow-basket, so she saw her own clothes, clean, dry, and neatly folded on the stool where she'd dropped her running shoes. She realized she hadn't even taken off the anklets before she got into bed. She wriggled her toes in them. No tenderness there. Her hands were stiff but cool, so Penda'd gotten out all the slivers. The skin of her left arm and leg was stiff, though, and she threw back the quilt and tried to see the injuries. She couldn't, but there was a little too much heat in the skin on the back of her left arm for her liking, and her right leg. Five sort-of-sore spots she couldn't really check at all other than identifying them as "sore." And, when she checked her legs, two bad red bumps on her thigh, one in the left calf and two on the fleshy part of her right leg by the shinbone. She had suffered more hurt than she'd realized. And stickle slivers could work their way through your flesh and into your blood. If one got to your heart, you could die from it. She groaned and rose. Shook out her legs, testing the feel of her muscles, and, thanks to Penda's massage, they didn't ache. She dressed and then carefully folded the quilt, placing it just as she'd found it on the bed.

Making her way back to the stairs, she passed the bathing room and heard the hum of masculine voices, then a laugh that was clearly from a female runner. As she came down the stairs, she was aware of the smell of roasting meats. Her stomach rumbled. One long narrow window lit the hall that led to the main room, and she gauged that she had slept most of the day. Perhaps she ought to have had a healer check out the scratches, but Penda knew what to do as well as any Hall-trained healer . . . probably better, since she was a station manager's mate.

"Now, here's a one who's prompt for her supper," Torlo said, calling the attention of the runners sitting around the room to Tenna's appearance. He introduced her. "Had a brush with Haligon early this morning," he added, and Tenna did not fail to note that this brash personage was known to them all from the nods and grimaces on their faces.

"I tol' Lord Groghe myself," one of the older runners said, nodding his head and looking solemn, "that there'd be an accident . . . then what'd he say to that? I asked him. Someone hurt because a wild lad won't respect what's our rights and propitty." Then he nodded directly at Tenna. "You aren't the only one he's knocked aside. Dinncha hear him coming?"

"Met him on the hill curve, she said," Torlo answered before Tenna could open her own mouth.

"Bad place, bad place. Runner can't see around it," a second man said, and nodded his sympathy to her. "See you've scratches? Penda put her good junk on ya?" Tenna nodded. "You'll be right then. I've seen your kin on the traces, haven't I? Betchur one of Fedri and Cesila's, aincha?" He smiled knowingly at the others. "You're prettier than she was and she was some pretty woman."

Tenna decided to ignore the compliment and admitted to her parentage. "Have you been through Station Ninety-Seven?"

"A time or two, a time or two," he said, grinning amiably. His runner's belt was covered with stitches.

Torlo had come up beside her and now took her left arm to peer at the side she couldn't really see well.

"Punctures," he said in a flat tone.

The other runners came to be sure his verdict was correct. They all nodded sagely and resumed their seats.

"Sometimes I wonder if all those berries're worth the risk of them slivers in spring," the veteran runner said.

"Worse time of the Turn to fall into them," she was told again.

"Misler, you run over to Healer Hall," Torlo said to one of them.

"Oh, I don't think that's necessary," Tenna said, because you had to pay healers and she then wouldn't have enough for good leathers.

"Being as how it was the Lord Holder's runner-beast knocked you in, he'll pay for it," Torlo said, sensing her reluctance and winking at her.

"One of these days he'll have to pay out blood money iffen he doesn't bring that Haligon up short and *make* him quit our traces. Did those shod hooves leave many holes?" another man asked her.

"No," she had to admit. "Surface sprang right back up."

"Hmmm, that's what it's supposed to do."

"But we don't need Haligon galloping up and down like traces was put there for *his* benefit."

Misler departed on his errand and then, after each runner spoke his or her name and home station, a glass of wine was poured for her. She started to demur but Torlo eyed her sternly.

"You're not on the run list this day, girl."

"I need to finish my first Cross," she said wistfully as she took the glass and found an empty seat.

"You will, lass, you will," the first man—Grolly— said so assuredly as he held his glass up that she was heartened. The others all seconded his words.

A few scratches and maybe the three-four punctures were not going to keep her from reaching the western seashore. She sipped her wine.

The runners who'd been bathing descended now and were served their wine by the time Misler came trotting back, a man in healer colors following behind, with a hop and a skip to keep up with his long-legged escort.

Beveny introduced himself and asked for Penda to join him—a nicety that pleased Tenna and gave her a very good opinion of the journeyman. The consultation was conducted right there in the main hall since the injuries were to visible portions of her body. And the other runners were genuinely interested in knowing the worst of her condition and offered suggestions, most of them knowledgeable as to which herbs should be used and how efficacious they had been on such and such an occasion. Beveny kept a grin on his face as if he was well used to runner chaffering. As he probably was.

"I think this one, and the two on your leg, may still have slivers in them," Beveny said at length. "Nothing a poultice won't draw out overnight, I'm sure."

There were approving nods and wise smiles from the audience. Poultices were then discussed again and at length and the appropriate one decided on. During this part of the consultation, Tenna was installed in a comfortable padded chair, a long stool affair attached to the front of it so her legs could stretch out. She'd never been fussed over so much in her life, but it was a runner thing: she'd seen her mother and father take the same personal care of anyone arriving at their station with an injury. But to be the center of so much attention—and at Fort Station—was embarrassing in the extreme for Tenna and she kept trying to discount the urgency of such minor wounds. She did offer her packet of her mother's poultice, and three of the runners remarked favorably on Cesila's famous poultice, but hers was clearly for bruises, not infections, so the healer told her to keep it for emergencies.

"Which I hope you won't have, of course," he said, smiling at her as he mixed—with the hot water Penda fetched—an aromatic concoction that everyone now in the room had to approve.

Keenly aware that she must be properly modest and forbearing, as well as brave, Tenna braced herself for the treatment. Hot poultices, however therapeutic, could be somewhat uncomfortable. Then the mixture was ready. With deft fingers, Healer Beveny deposited neat blobs, no larger than his thumbnail, on the sore spots. He must have judged the heat just right, because none was too hot. He made sure to position the patches right over each blob before securing them with bandage strips that Penda had produced. Tenna felt each of the ten hot spots, but the sensation was not all that unpleasant.

"I'll check tomorrow, Tenna, but I don't think we have to worry about any of them," Beveny said with such conviction that Tenna was relieved.

"Nor do you, here at Fort Station with the Healer Hall a stretch away," said Torlo, and courteously saw Beveny to the door and watched a polite few moments until the healer was halfway to his Hall.

"Nice fella," he said to anyone listening, and smiled at Tenna. "Ah, here's the food."

Evidently that meal had been held up for her to

be treated, because now Penda led in the drudge carrying the roast platter with others behind him, laden with large bowls of steaming food.

"Rosa," she said, pointing to one of the female runners, "get the board. Spacia, grab a fork and spoon for Tenna. She's not to move. Grolly, her glass is empty. . . ." As she directed the others to serve the injured runner, she herself carved fine slices from the roasted ribs of herdbeast. "The rest of you, get on line."

Tenna's embarrassment returned, waited on as she was by Rosa and Spacia, who cheerfully performed their assigned tasks. Always she had been the one to help, so this situation was quite novel. Of course, it was also a runner thing, to be cosseted in need, but she'd never been the recipient before.

Two more batches of runners arrived in from south and east. When they came back from bathing, they had to be told all about Haligon's forcing Tenna off the trace and how she had sticklebush punctures that were severe enough to require a healer. She got the distinct impression that almost everyone had had a run-in with this infamous Haligon, or knew someone who had. Eventually the tale had been told to everyone and the conversation changed to talk of the Gather three days hence.

Tenna sighed softly to herself. Three days? She'd be fully recovered by then and have to run on. She really did want to get the extra stitches for her first Cross. A Gather, even one at Fort, was not as important as upgrading herself. Well, nearly. It wasn't as if this were the last Gather she'd ever have a chance to attend, even if it was the first for her at the First Hold on Pern.

This was home station for two girls. Rosa had a cap of very tight dark curls and a pert face with mischievous eyes. Spacia, with long blond hair tied back, runner-wise, had a more dignified way about her although she kept up a wickedly bantering conversation with the younger male runners among others there. Then there was an informal concert for Tenna, some of the newer songs that the Harper Hall was airing. Rosa led, Spacia adding an alto line while three of the other runners joined in, one with a little whistle and the others with their voices. The evening became quite enjoyable, especially as either Grolly or Torlo kept filling Tenna's wineglass.

Rosa and Spacia helped her up the stairs, one on either side of her, with the excuse that the bandages mustn't loosen. They chattered about what they intended to wear to the Gather and who they hoped to dance with.

"We're on line tomorrow," Rosa said as they got her to her bed, "so we'll probably be off before you get down. Those poultices ought to do the trick."

They both wished her a good night's sleep. Her head was spinning as she lay down, but pleasantly, and she drifted into sleep very quickly.

Torlo arrived with a tray of food just as she was waking up.

"Not as sore today?"

"Not all over but my leg . . ." She pulled the quilt back so he could see.

"Hmmm. Need more on that one. Went in at an angle. I'm calling Beveny."

"Oh, really . . . I'd rather . . . Surely Penda knows what the healer made up for me . . ."

"She does, but we want the healer to speak about your injuries to Lord Groghe."

Tenna was dismayed now. A runner didn't go to the Lord Holder without *real* cause for complaint, and her injuries were not that serious.

"Now, see here, young runner," and Torlo waggled a finger at her, "I'm station master and I say we take this to the Lord Holder on account of it shouldna happened at all."

Beveny recommended a long soak in the tub and provided her with an astringent to use in the water.

"I'll leave more poultice with Penda. We want that final sliver out. See . . ." and he pointed to the thin, almost invisible hairs of the sticklebush which had come from the arm puncture. "We want another of these fellows on the pad, not in you."

Two more had also erupted from the puncture wounds, and he carefully covered all three pads with glass slides, which he tied together.

"Soak at least an hour, Tenna," he told her. "You're to take it very handy today, too. Don't want that sliver to work any farther down in your flesh."

She shuddered at the thought of an evil-looking hair loose in her body.

"Don't worry. It'll be out by evening," Beveny said, grinning reassuringly. "And you'll be dancing with us."

"Oh, I'll have to run on as soon as I'm able," she said earnestly.

Beveny's grin broadened. "What? And do me out of my dance with you?" Then his expression turned professional. "I can't release you as fit to run yet, you know. I'd want to see those puncture marks healing. Especially in the shin, where just the dirt and dust of a run could be embedded and cause a repeat infection. The wounds may seem," and he emphasized the word, "insignificant but I've tended a lot of runners and I know the hazards of the trace."

"Oh," Tenna said meekly.

"Right. Oh!" And he grinned again, pressing her shoulder with a kindly squeeze. "You will make your first Cross. Now rest. You runners are a breed apart, you know."

With that reminder, he left her to make her way to the bathing room.

Rosa, Spacia, Grolly—in fact, all the runners at the Fort Station—were in and out, groaning over the special messages that needed to be delivered to the Fort crafthalls, the Lord Holder, the Harper Hall, coming from the "backside of beyond" as Rosa termed it.

"Don't mind us," Rosa said when Tenna began to feel as if she ought to be doing her share. "It's always like this just before a Gather and we always complain, but the Gather makes up for it. Which reminds me, you don't have anything to wear."

"Oh, no, don't worry about me...."

"Nonsense," Spacia said. "We will if we want to

and we do." She gave Tenna's long frame an intent look and then shook her head. "Well, nothing we have would fit." Both girls were shorter than Tenna by a full head and, while neither carried much flesh, they were stockier than the eastern girl.

Then both turned to each other in the same instant and snapped their fingers. "Silvina!" they exclaimed in chorus.

"C'mon," Spacia said, and reached for Tenna's hand. "You can walk, can't you?"

"Oh, yes, but . . ."

"On your feet then, runner," Rosa said, and took Tenna's other arm, assisting her to an upright position. "Silvina's headwoman at the Harper Hall and she always has good things. . . ."

"But . . . I . . ." and then Tenna gave up protesting. It was obvious from the determined expressions on the two runners' faces that they would brook no argument.

"You're taking her to Silvina?" Penda asked, sidling out of the kitchen. "Good. I've nothing here to fit her and she's got to look her best when she meets that wretch Haligon."

"Why?" Tenna suspiciously wanted to know. Why would she need to look her best just to give Haligon what-for?

"Why, to maintain the reputation of Fort Station, of course," Rosa said with an impish grin. "We've our pride, you know, and you may be a visitor but you're here, now," and she pointed emphatically to the ground, "and must be presentable."

"Not that you aren't," Spacia hastily added, being slightly more tactful than Rosa, "except we want you more so than ever."

"After all, it *is* your first Fort Gather..."

"And you nearly finishing your first Cross, too."

Their chatter was impossible to resist and there was no way Tenna could appear at a Gather in runner gear, which was all she had of her own to wear.

At this evening hour, they found Silvina checking day-records in her office at the Harper Hall and she was more than delighted that she had been approached. She led them down to the storage rooms underneath the Harper Hall.

"We keep quite a few performance dresses in case a soloist wants to wear harper colors. You wouldn't mind wearing blue, would you?" Silvina said as she paused by the second of a line of locked doors. "Actually, I think blue would be a very good color for you." She had such a lovely speaking voice that Tenna was listening more to her tone than what she was saying. "And I've one that I think might be just the thing for you."

She opened a large wardrobe and, from the many there, she brought out a long gown with full sleeves and some fine embroidered trim that made all three girls gasp.

"It's lovely. Oh, I couldn't wear something this valuable," Tenna exclaimed, backing away.

"Nonsense," Silvina said, and gestured for Tenna to slip out of her runner top.

When Tenna carefully slipped on the dress, the softness of the fabric against her skin made her feel . . . special. She tried a little spin and the long skirt swirled about her ankles while the full sleeves billowed about her arms. It was the most flattering dress she'd worn and she examined it thoroughly, committing the details of its design to her mind so that she could reproduce it the next time she had marks enough for a Gather dress. The one she had at home was nowhere near as splendid as this. Could she, should she dance, in something as elegant as this? What if she spilled something on it?

"I'm not sure . . . ," she began as she faced her companions.

"Not *sure!*" Rosa was indignant. "Why, that deep blue shows up your lovely skin and your eyes . . .

they are blue, aren't they, or is it the dress makes them so? And it fits like it was made for *you!*"

Tenna looked down at the low-cut front of the bodice. Whoever it had been made for had had a lot more breast. She didn't fill it out properly. Silvina was rummaging through another box.

"Here," she said, and stuffed two pads in the front, settling them with such a practiced hand that the adjustment was done before Tenna could protest.

"*There!* That's much better," Spacia said, and then giggled. "I have to pad, too. But it'd be worse for us as runners to be heavy, bumping around all the time."

Tenna tentatively felt her newly improved form but, as she looked at herself in the mirror, she could see that the fit of the top was vastly improved and she looked more ... more ... well, it fit better. The fabric was so smooth to the touch, it was a pleasure just to feel the dress on her. And this shade of blue ...

"This is Harper blue," she said with surprise.

"Of course it is," Silvina said with a laugh. "Not that it matters. You'll be wearing runner cords ... though right now," and Silvina's appreciative grin broadened, "you don't look runnerish ... if you'll forgive my frankness."

Tenna couldn't help admiring how much better her

figure looked with that little alteration. She had a slim waist and the dress hugged it before flaring out over hips that she knew to be too bony and best covered.

"The pads won't ... pop out ... will they, when I'm dancing?"

"If you'll take off the dress, I'll put a few stitches to secure them where they should stay," Silvina said.

That was done so quickly that Silvina was folding the lovely dress over Tenna's arm before she realized it.

"Now, shoes?" Spacia asked. "She can't wear spikes...."

"She might better wear them," Rosa said dourly, "with some of those louts who come to a Fort Gather. Haligon's not the only one who'll home in on her, looking that way."

Silvina had cast a measuring glance at Tenna's long, narrow feet and now took a long box down from one of the many shelves in this huge storeroom.

"Should have something to fit even narrow runner feet ... ," she murmured, and came up with a pair of soft, ankle-high, black suede boots. "Try these."

They did not fit. But the fourth pair—in dark red—were only slightly too long.

"Wear thick anklets and they'll fit fine," Spacia suggested.

And the three girls left, Tenna carefully transporting the dress to the station. Rose and Spacia insisted on sharing the burden of the boots and the underskirt that Silvina had offered to complete the costume.

The last sliver of sticklebush was on the pad the next morning and Beveny added it to the others, handing the evidence packet over to Torlo, who grinned in satisfaction.

"This'll make Lord Groghe see that we've a legitimate complaint," he said, and nodded emphatically at Tenna. She was about to protest when he added, "But not until after the Gather, for he's too busy to be approached right now. And he'll be in a much better mood after a good Gather." He turned to Tenna. "So you have to stay till after and that's that."

"But I could run short distances now, couldn't I?"

"Mmm," Torlo said, nodding. "Iffen a run comes up. Don't like to be idle, do you, girl?" She shook her head. "Wal, Healer, is she fit?"

"Short run and no hills," Beveny said, "and nowhere Haligon might ride." He grinned mischievously at her and took his leave.

Just before midday, Torlo called her from the front bench where she'd been watching the Gather stalls being erected.

"Run down to the port for me, will you? A ship just was drummed in and has cargo for the Gather. We're to get its manifests." He took her by the arm and showed the route to her on the big map of Fort Hold that displayed local traces and roads. "Straight run ... downhill all the way to the port. And not too steep on the way back."

It was good to be running again and, though the spring weather had turned chilly, she soon worked up enough heat to keep warm. The captain was much relieved to deliver the manifests to her. The cargo was being unloaded and he was anxious to get it up the road to the Hold in time for the Gather. He was equally anxious to receive payment for the deliveries, and she could promise she'd have the manifests in the designated hands before dinnertime.

He also had a pouch of letters from the eastern seacoast on board which were addressed to Fort Hold. So she carried a full belt back. Her legs felt the slight incline but she didn't decrease her pace despite a slight soreness in the right leg at the shin.

Well, a warm bath in one of those incredible

tubs would take care of that. And the Gather was
tomorrow.

Fort Station was full that night, with runners coming from other stations for the Gather the next day.
Tenna bunked in with Rosa and Spacia and a southern runner, Delfie, took the fourth bed in their
room. It was a front room with a window, and you
heard the traffic on the road, but Tenna was tired
enough to sleep through anything.

"Which is as well because the comings and goings up the main track kept up all night long," Rosa
said with cheerful disgust. "Let's eat outside. It's so
crowded in here." So they all sat on the front
benches to eat.

Spacia gave Tenna a conspiratorial wink as Tenna
followed the others outside. There had been a few
spare seats but not all together. It would be nicer to
eat outside instead of at the packed tables. Penda
and her drudges had their hands full pouring klah
and distributing bread, cheese, and porridge.

Actually, it was much more interesting to sit outside to eat. There was so much going on. Gather wagons kept arriving from both directions and rolled
onto the field set aside for their use. Stalls which had

been bare boards and uprights last night were being decorated with Hall colors and craft insignia. And more stalls were being erected on the wide court in front of the Hold. The long tongue-and-groove boards for the dancing surface were being slotted into place in the center and the harpers' platform erected. Tenna wanted to hug herself with delight at all the activity. She'd never actually seen a Gather gathering before . . . especially in such a big Hold as Fort. Since she had run yesterday, she felt a little better about not having made a push to finish her first Cross. And she had the chance to see the dragonriders pop into the air above Fort Hold.

"Oh, they are so beautiful," she said, noticing that Rosa and Spacia were also watching the graceful creatures landing, and the elegantly clad dragonriders dismounting.

"Yes, they are," Rosa said in an odd tone. "I just wish they wouldn't keep going on about Thread coming back." She shuddered.

"You don't think it will?" Tenna said, for she had recently had several runs into the Benden Station and knew that weyrfolk were certain that Thread would return. Hadn't the

Red Star been seen in the Eye Rock at the winter solstice?

Rosa shrugged. "It can for all of me but it's going to interfere with running something fierce."

"I noticed that the Benden Thread halts are all repaired," Tenna said.

Spacia shrugged. "We'd be fools to take any chances, wouldn't we?" Then she grimaced. "I'd really hate to be stuck in one of those boxes with Thread falling all around me. Why, the wardrobe in Silvina's storeroom is larger. What if it got in a crack, Thread got in, and I couldn't get out?" She pantomimed terror and revulsion.

"It'll never come to that," Rosa said confidently.

"Lord Groghe certainly got rid of all the greenery around the Hold," Spacia remarked, gesturing around.

"That was as much for the Gather as because the dragonriders said he had to," Rosa said dismissively. "Oh, here come the Boll runners. . . ." She jumped to her feet, waving at the spearhead of runners who had just appeared on the southern road.

They were running effortlessly, their legs moving as if they had drilled that matched stride. They certainly made a fine sight, Tenna thought, pride swelling in her chest and catching her breath.

"They must have started last night," Rosa said. "Oh, d'you see Cleve, Spacia?"

"Third rank from the rear," Spacia said pointing. "As if anyone could miss *him!*" she added in a slightly derisive tone, winking at Tenna. Then she murmured, behind her hand for Tenna's ears only, "She's been so sure he wouldn't come . . . Ha!"

Tenna grinned, now understanding why Rosa had wanted to sit outside that morning and why she had sent Spacia in when they needed more klah.

Then, all of a sudden, as if the arrival of that contingent had been the signal, the Gather was ready. All stalls were up and furnished, the first shift of harpers on the platform and ready to entertain. Then Rosa pointed to the wide steps leading down from the entrance to the Hold and there were the Lord and Lady, looking exceedingly grand in brown Gather finery, descending to the court to formally open the Gather Square. They were accompanied by the dragonriders as well as a clutch of folk, young and old and all related to the Lord Holder. According to Rosa, Lord Groghe had a large family.

"Oh, let's not miss the opening," Spacia told Tenna. Rosa had accompanied Cleve into the station and was helping Penda serve the Boll group a second breakfast after their long run.

So the two girls had excellent seats to watch the two Lord Holders do the official walk through the Gather.

"There's Haligon," Spacia said, her tone hard, pointing.

"Which one?"

"He's wearing brown," Spacia said.

Tenna was none the wiser. "There are a lot of people wearing brown."

"He's walking just behind Lord Groghe."

"So are a lot of other people."

"He's got the curliest head of hair," Spacia added.

There were two who answered that description, but Tenna decided it was the shorter of the young men, the one who walked with a definite swagger. That had to be Haligon. He was handsome enough, though she liked the appearance of the taller man in brown more: not as attractive perhaps, but with a nicer grin on his face. Haligon obviously thought himself very much the lad, from the smug expression on *his* face.

Tenna nodded. She'd give him what-for, so she would.

"C'mon, we should change before the mob gets upstairs," Spacia said, touching Tenna's arm to get her attention.

Now that she had identified Haligon, Tenna was quite ready to be looking her very best. Spacia was also determined to assist and took pains with Tenna's appearance, fluffing her hair so that it framed her face, helping her with lip color and a touch of eye shadow.

"Bring out the blue in 'em, though your eyes are really gray, aren't they?"

"Depends on what I'm wearing." Tenna gave a little twirl in front of the long mirror in the room, watching the bias-cut swirl around her ankles. As Spacia had suggested, the anklets took up the spare room in the toes of the borrowed boots. Nor did they look ungainly on the end of her legs as her long feet usually did. She was really quite pleased with her looks. And had to admit, with a degree of satisfaction, that she looked "pretty."

Then Spacia stood beside her, the yellow of her gown an attractive contrast to Tenna's deep blue.

"Oops, I'd better find you some spare runner cords or everyone'll think you're new in the Harper Hall."

No spare cords were found, though Spacia turned out all the drawers.

"Maybe I should be Harper Hall," Tenna said

thoughtfully. "That way I can deal with Haligon as he deserves before he suspects."

"Hmm, that might be the wiser idea, you know," Spacia agreed.

Rosa came rushing in, pulling at her clothes in a rush to change.

"Need any help?" Spacia asked as Rosa pulled her pink, floral-printed Gather dress from its hanger.

"No, no but get down there and keep Felisha from Cleve. She's determined to get him, you know. Waltzed right in before he'd finished eating and started hanging on his arm as if they were espoused." Rosa's voice was muffled as she pulled the dress over her head. They all heard a little tearing and Rosa cried out in protest, standing completely still, the dress half on. "Oh, no, no! What did I rip? What'll I do? How bad is it? Can you see?"

While the seam had only parted a bit, and Spacia was threading a needle to make the repairs, Rosa was so disturbed at the thought of her rival that Tenna volunteered to go down.

"You know which one Cleve is?" Rosa asked anxiously, and Tenna nodded and left the room.

She identified Felisha before she did Cleve. The girl, with a mop of curly black tangles half covering her face, was flirting outrageously with the tall, lantern-jawed runner. He had an engaging smile, though a trifle absent, as he kept looking toward the stairs. Tenna chuckled to herself. Rosa needn't worry. Cleve was obviously uncomfortable with Felisha's coy looks and the way she kept tossing her hair over her shoulder, letting it flick into his face.

"Cleve?" she asked as she approached them. Felisha glared at her and gave her head a perceptible tilt to indicate to Tenna to move on.

"Yes?" Cleve moved a step closer to Tenna, and farther from Felisha, who then altered her stance to put her arm through his in a proprietary fashion that obviously annoyed Cleve.

"Rosa told me that you'd had a run-in with Haligon, too?"

"Yes, I did," Cleve said, seizing on the subject and trying to disentangle himself. "Ran me down on the Boll trace six sevendays ago. Got a nasty sprain out of it. Rosa mentioned he pushed you into sticklebush and you had some mean slivers. Caught you on the hill curve, did he?"

Tenna turned up her hands to show the mottled sliver pricks still visible from that encounter.

"How terrible!" Felisha said insincerely. "That boy's far too reckless."

"Indeed," Tenna said, not liking this girl at all,

though she smiled amiably. Surely she was too heavy-set to be a runner. Her mop of hair covered whatever Hall or Hold cords she might be wearing. Tenna turned to Cleve. "Spacia told me that you know a lot about the local leathers and I need new shoes."

"Don't they tan hides wherever you come from?" Felisha asked snidely.

"Station Ninety-Seven, isn't it?" Cleve said, grinning. "Come, I've a mind to look for new leathers myself and the bigger the Gather the more chance at a good price, right?" He brushed free of Felisha and, taking Tenna by the arm, propelled her across to the door.

Tenna had a brief glance at the furious look on Felisha's face as they made their escape.

"Thank *you*, Tenna," Cleve said, exhaling with exaggeration as they strode across the court to the Gather Square. "That girl's a menace."

"Is she a Boll runner? She didn't introduce herself."

Cleve chuckled. "No, she's Weaver Hall," he said dismissively, "but my station runs messages for her Craftmaster." He grimaced.

"Tenna?" Torlo called from the door, and they both stopped, allowing him to catch up with them.

"Anyone point out Haligon to you yet?" he asked.

"Yes, Rosa and Spacia did. He was behind the Lord Holder. I'll have a word with him when we meet."

"Good girl, good girl," Torlo said, pressing her arm firmly in encouragement, and then he returned to the station.

"Will you?" Cleve asked, eyes wide with surprise.

"Will I what? Give him what-for? Indeed I will," Tenna said, firming her mind with purpose. "A bit of what he gave me."

"I thought it was sticklebushes you fell into?" Cleve asked, taking it all literally. "There're none of those in a Square."

"Measuring his length on a Gather floor will do nicely, I think," she replied. It ought to be rather easy to trip someone up with such a crowd around. And she had committed herself rather publicly to giving this Haligon a visible lesson. Even Healer Beveny was helping her. She was obliged to act. She certainly didn't wish to lose respect in the station. She took a deep breath. Would tripping him be sufficient? At least on the personal level. There'd still be the charge of reckless behavior leveled against him

with the healer-verified proof of her injuries. These had certainly kept her from
running for three days—loss of income.

"Oh!" she said, seeing the display for fab-
rics draped on the Weaver Hall booth: bril-
liant colors, and floral prints, as well as
stripes in both bold and muted colors. She
put her hands behind her back because the
temptation to finger the cloth was almost ir-
resistible.

Cleve wrinkled his nose. "That's Felisha's
Hall's stuff."

"Oh, that red is amazing. . . ."

"Yeah, it's a good Hall. . . ."

"In spite of her?" Tenna chuckled at his
reluctant admission.

"Yes . . ." and he grinned ruefully.

They passed the Glasscraft display: mir-
rors with ornate frames and plain wood,
goblets and drinking glasses in all shapes and
colors, pitchers in all sizes.

Tenna caught a reflection and almost
didn't recognize herself except for that fact
that there was Cleve beside her. She straightened her shoulders and smiled back at the
unfamiliar girl in the glass.

The next stand was a large Tailor Hall display with finished goods in tempting array: dresses, shirts, trousers, and more intimate garments— enticing merchandise, to be sure, and this one was already packed out with buyers.

"What's keeping Rosa?" Cleve asked, glancing back over his shoulder toward the station, which would be visible until they turned the corner.

"Well, she wanted to look extra nice for you," Tenna said.

Cleve grinned. "She always looks nice." And he blushed suddenly.

"She's a very kind and thoughtful person," Tenna said sincerely.

"Ah, here we are," he said, pointing to the hides displayed at the stall on the corner of the square. "Though I think there are several stalls. Fort Gathers're big enough to attract a lot of crafthalls. Let's see what's available everyplace. Are you good at haggling? If you're not, we can leave it to Rosa. She's very good. And they'd know she means business. You being unknown, they might think they could put one over on you."

Tenna grinned slyly. "I plan to get the most for my mark, I assure you."

"I shouldn't teach you how to run traces, then,

should I?" Cleve said with a tinge of rueful apology in his voice.

Tenna smiled back and began to saunter aimlessly past the leather stall. Just then Rosa caught up with them, giving Tenna a kiss as if they hadn't parted company fifteen minutes before. Cleve threw one arm about Rosa's shoulders and whispered in her ear, making her giggle. Other shoppers walked around the three, standing in the middle of the wide aisle. Tenna didn't object to the chance to examine the leather goods without appearing to do so. The journeyman behind the counter pretended not to see her not looking at his wares. She was also trying to see if she could spot Haligon among those promenading about the Square.

By the time the three of them had done their first circuit of the Gather, it was almost impossible to move for the crowds. But a goodly crowd also added to the "Gather feeling," and the trio of runners were exhilarated by the atmosphere. They spent so many hours in work that was solitary and time-consuming, often at hours when most other folk had finished their labors and were enjoying companionship and family life. True, they had the constant satisfaction of knowing that they provided an important service, but you didn't think of that running through a chilling rain or battling against a fierce gale. You thought more of what you *didn't* have and what you were missing.

Refreshment stalls displayed all kinds of drink and finger edibles. So, when they had finished their circuit, they bought food and drink and sat at the tables about the dance square.

"There he is!" Rosa said suddenly, pointing across the square to where a group of young men were surveying girls parading in their Gather finery. It was a custom to take a Gather partner, someone with whom to spend the occasion—which could include the day, the evening meal, the dancing, and whatever else was mutually decided. Everyone recognized the limitation and made sure that the details were arranged ahead of time so that there wouldn't be a misunderstanding of intent.

This would be an ideal situation in which to make Haligon suffer indignity. The area where he was standing with his friends was at the roadside, dusty and spotted with droppings from all the draft animals pulling Gather wagons past it. He'd look silly, his good clothes mussed. With any luck, she could get his fancy Gather clothing soiled as well as dusty.

"Excuse me," Tenna said, putting down her drink. "I've a score to settle."

"Oh!" Rosa's eyes went wide but an encouraging "yo-ho" followed Tenna as she cut diagonally across the wooden dancing floor.

Haligon was still in the company of the taller man, laughing at something said and eyeing the girls who were parading conspicuously along that side of the Gather Square. Yes, this was the time to repay him for her fall.

Tenna went right up to him, tapped him on the shoulder, and when he turned around in response, the arch smile on his face turned to one of considerable interest at her appearance, his eyes lighting as he gave her a sweeping look of appreciation. He was looking so boldly that he did not see Tenna cock her right arm. Putting her entire body into the swing, she connected her fist smartly to his chin. He dropped like a felled herdbeast, flat on his back and unconscious. And right on top of some droppings. Although the impact of her fist on his chin had rocked her back on her heels, she brushed her hands together with great satisfaction and, pivoting on the heel of her borrowed red shoe, retraced her steps.

She was halfway back to Rosa and Cleve when she heard someone rapidly overtaking her. So she

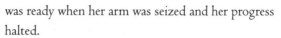

was ready when her arm was seized and her progress halted.

"What was that all about?" It was the tall lad in brown who pulled her about, a look of genuine surprise on his face. And his eyes, too, surveyed her in her formfitting blue dress.

"I thought he ought to have a little of what he deals out so recklessly," she said, and proceeded.

"Wait a minute. What was he supposed to have done to you? I've never seen you around Fort before and he's never mentioned meeting someone like you. And he would!" His eyes glinted with appreciation.

"Oh?" Tenna cocked her head at him. They were nearly at eye level. "Well, he pushed me into sticklebushes." She showed him her hands and his expression altered to one of real concern.

"Sticklebushes? They're dangerous at this season."

"I do know that . . . the hard way," she replied caustically.

"But where? When?"

"That doesn't matter. I've evened the score."

"Indeed," and his grin was respectful. "But are you sure it was my brother?"

"Do you know all Haligon's friends?"

"Haligon?" He blinked. After a pause in which

his eyes reflected a rapid series of considerations, he said, "I thought I did." And he laughed nervously. Then he gestured for her to continue on her way. She could see that he was being careful not to annoy her, and that provided her with further amused satisfaction.

"There is a lot about Haligon that he would want kept quiet," she said. "He's a reckless sort."

"And you're the one to teach him manners?" He had to cover his mouth, but she could see that his eyes were brimming with laughter.

"Someone has to."

"Oh? Just what offense did he give you? It's not often . . . Haligon . . . measures his length. Couldn't you have found a less public spot to deliver your lesson? You've ruined his Gather clothes with muck."

"Actually, I chose the spot deliberately. Let him feel what it's like to be flattened unexpectedly."

"Yes, I'm sure. But where did you encounter him?"

"He was using a runner trace, at a gallop, in the middle of the night. . . ."

"Oh," and he stopped dead in his tracks, an odd, almost guilty look on his face. "When was this?" he asked, all amusement gone.

"Four nights ago, at the hill curve."

"And?"

"I was knocked into sticklebushes." With those words, she held out her right leg and pulled her skirt up high enough to expose the red dots of the healing injuries. And again displayed her free hand and its healing rack of punctures.

"They got infected?" He was really concerned now and obviously knew the dangers of the sticklebush.

"I've saved the slivers," she said in a firm tone. "Healer Beveny has them for proof. I wasn't able to continue working and I've been laid up three days."

"I'm sorry to hear that." And he sounded sincere, his expression somber. Then he gave his head a little shake and smiled at her, a trifle warily, but there was a look in his eyes that told her he found her attractive. "If you promise not to drop me, may I say that you don't look at all like most runners I've met." His eyes lingered only briefly on her bodice, and then he hastily cleared his throat. "I'd better get back and see . . . if Haligon's come to."

Tenna spared a glance at the little knot of people clustered around her victim and, giving him a gracious nod, continued on her way back to Rosa and Cleve.

They were looking pale and shocked.

"There! Honor is satisfied," she said, slipping into her seat.

Rosa and Cleve exchanged looks.

"No," Rosa said, and leaned toward her, one hand on her forearm. "It wasn't Haligon you knocked down."

"It wasn't? But that's the fellow you pointed out to me. He's in brown . . ."

"So is Haligon. He's the one followed you across the dance floor. The one you were talking to, and I don't think you were giving him any what-for."

"Oh." Tenna slumped weakly against the back of her chair. "I hit the wrong man?"

"Uh-huh," Rosa said as both she and Cleve nodded their heads.

"Oh dear," and she made a start to get up but Rosa hastily put out a restraining hand.

"I don't think apologies will help."

"No? Who did I hit?"

"His twin brother, Horon, who's bad enough in his own way."

"Quite likely, with the lewd look he gave me." Tenna was halfway to convincing herself that she had at least hit someone who needed a put-down.

"Horon's a bit of a bully and nice girls won't have anything to do with him. Especially at a Gather."

Then Rosa giggled, covering her mouth with her hand. "He was sure looking you up and down. That's why we thought you'd hit him."

Remembering the force of her punch, Tenna rubbed her sore knuckles.

"You may have done someone a favor," Cleve said, grinning. "That was some punch."

"My brothers taught me how," Tenna said absently, watching the group across the Square. She was a trifle relieved when Horon was helped to his feet. And pleased that he staggered and needed assistance. Then, as the group around Horon moved about, she saw Haligon's figure striding up to the station. "Uh-oh. Why's he going to the station?"

"I wouldn't worry about that," Rosa said, standing up. "Torlo would love to remind him of all the harm he's been doing runners."

"Even if they weren't as pretty as you are," Cleve said. "Let's see about your leathers."

They took their empty glasses back to the refreshment stand. Tenna managed one more look at the station but there was no sign of Haligon or Torlo, though there was a lot of coming and going. There would be, on a Gather day. Would she have to knock Haligon down, too? To satisfy runner honor? It wouldn't be as easy, for he had been wary enough of her when he had caught up with her on the dance floor.

After a second round of the Gather stalls, they all decided to find out what prices were being asked. At the first tanner's stall, Cleve did more of the talking so that the real buyer was protected from the blandishments of the tanner journeyman, a man named Ligand.

"Blue for a harper singer?" Ligand had begun, glancing at Tenna. "Thought I saw you eyeing the stall earlier."

"I'm runner," Tenna said.

"She just happens to look her best in blue," Rosa said quickly in case Tenna might be embarrassed to admit she wore a borrowed gown.

"She does indeed," Ligand said, "I'd never have guessed her for a runner."

"Why not?" Rosa asked, bridling.

"Because she's wearing blue," Ligand said deferentially. "So what color is your delight this fine Gather day?"

"I'd like a dark green," and Tenna pointed to a stack of hides dyed various shades of that color in the shelves behind him.

"Good choice for a runner," he said and, with a deft lift, transferred the heavy stack of hides to the front counter. Then he moved off to the other end of his stall, where two holders were examining heavy belts.

"Not that trace moss leaves stains," Rosa remarked as Tenna began flipping through the pile, fingering the leather as she went along.

"We go for the reddy-browns in Boll," Cleve said. "So much of the soil down in Boll is that shade. And trace moss doesn't do as well in the heat as it does in the north."

"Does fine in Igen," Tenna said, having run trace there.

"So it does," Cleve said reflectively. "I like that one," he added, spreading his hand over the hide before Tenna could flip to the next one. "Good deep emerald green."

Tenna had also been considering it. "Enough here for boots. I only need enough for summer shoes. He wouldn't want to divide it."

"Ah, and you've found one you like, huh? Good price on that." Ligand was obviously aware of all that went on at his booth. He flipped up the hide to see the markings on the underside. "Give it to you for nine marks."

Rosa gasped. "At five it's robbery." Then she

looked chagrined to have protested when Tenna was the prospective purchaser.

"I'd agree with that," Tenna said, having only four to spend. She gave the skin one more pat and, smiling courteously at Ligand, walked off, her companions hastily following her.

"You won't find better quality anywhere," Ligand called after them.

"It was good quality," Tenna murmured as they walked away. "But four marks is my limit."

"Oh, we should be able to find a smaller hide for that much, though maybe not the same green," Rosa said airily.

However, by the time they had done a third circuit and seen all the green hides available, they had not found either the same green or the same beautifully softened hide.

"I just don't have five, even if we could bargain him down to that price," Tenna said. "That brown at the third stand would be all right. Shall we try that?"

"Oho," Rosa said, stopping in her tracks, her expression alarmed.

Cleve, too, was stopped, and Tenna couldn't see what caused their alarm until suddenly a man appeared out of the crowd and stood directly in their path. She recognized the tall, white-haired man from the morning's ceremony as Lord Holder Groghe.

"Runner Tenna?" he asked formally. But the expression in his wide-set eyes was pleasant.

"Yes," she said, raising her chin slightly. Was he about to give *her* what-for for punching his son Horon? She certainly couldn't admit to having hit the wrong one.

"Shall we sit over here, with your friends?" Lord Groghe said, gesturing toward a free table. He put a hand on her elbow and guided her gently in that direction, away from the stream of folk.

Tenna thought confusedly that neither his expression nor his tone was peremptory. He was unexpectedly gracious. A heavyset man with a full face and the beginning of jowls, he smiled to everyone as they made their way to the table, for there were many curious glances at the four of them. He caught the eye of the wineman and held up four fingers. The wineman nodded and hastened to serve them.

"I have an apology to make to you, Runner Tenna." He kept his voice low and for their ears alone.

"You do?" And, at Rosa's startled expression, Tenna added courteously with only a short hesitation, "Lord Groghe?"

"I have verified that my son, Haligon, ran you down four nights ago and you were sufficiently injured so that you were unable to run." Groghe's brows met in a scowl that was for the circumstances, not her part in them. "I confess that I have heard rumors of other complaints about his use of runner traces. Station Master Torlo informed me of several near-collisions. You may be sure that, from now on, Haligon will leave the traces for the runners who made them. You're from Station Ninety-Seven? Keroon Hold?"

Tenna could only nod. She couldn't believe this was happening. A Lord Holder was apologizing to her?

"My son, Haligon, had no idea that he had nearly run you down the other night. He may be reckless," and Groghe smiled somewhat indulgently, "but he would never knowingly cause injury."

Rosa prodded Tenna in the ribs, and Tenna realized that she must make as much as she could of this opportunity, not just for herself but for all runners.

"Lord Groghe, I . . . we all," and she included

Rosa and Cleve, "would be grateful to know that we may run the traces without interference. I had only the briefest warning that someone else was using the path. The hill hid his approach and there was wind, too, covering the sound. I could have been severely injured. Traces are not wide you know." He nodded, and she went on boldly. "And they were made for runners, not riders." He nodded again. "I think Fort Station would be grateful for your help in keeping just runners on the traces."

Then she couldn't think of anything else to say. And just sat there smiling with nervous twitches in the corners of her mouth.

"I have been well and truly told off, Runner Tenna." He smiled back at her, his eyes dropping for a split second to her bodice. "You're a very pretty girl. Blue becomes you." He reached over and gave her hand a pat before he rose. "I've told Torlo that the incursions will cease." Then, in his usual booming voice, he added, "Enjoy the Gather, runners, and the wine."

With that he rose and walked off, nodding and smiling as he went, leaving the three runners stunned. Rosa was the first to recover. She took a good swig of the wine.

"Torlo was right. You did it," Rosa said. "And this is *good* wine."

"What else would they serve Lord Groghe?" Cleve said, and surreptitiously eased the glass left at the Lord Holder's seat closer to his. The level of wine had not been much reduced by the sip that Lord Groghe had taken. "We can split this one."

"I can't believe that Lord Holder apologized to . . ." Tenna shook her head, hand on her chest. ". . . me. Tenna."

"You were the one injured, weren't you?" Rosa said.

"Yes, but . . ."

"How did Lord Groghe know?" Cleve finished for Tenna, who was puzzling such an answer.

"We all saw Haligon go up to the station," Rosa said before taking another sip of the wine. She rolled her eyes in appreciation of the taste. "But Lord Groghe's a fair man, even if he usually thinks women are half-wits. But he's fair." Then she giggled again. "And he said how pretty you are, so that helped, you know. Haligon likes his girls pretty. So does Lord Groghe but he only looks."

The three runners had been so intent on their own conversation that they did not notice Haligon's approach until he unrolled the green hide from Ligand's stall in front of Tenna.

"In apology, Runner Tenna, because I really didn't know there was someone on the curve of the trace the other night," Haligon said, and gave a courteous bow, his eyes fixed on Tenna's face. Then his contrite expression altered to chagrin. "The station master gave me what-for in triples. So did my father."

"Oh, didn't you believe Tenna?" Rosa asked him pertly.

"How could I doubt the injuries she showed me?" Haligon said. Now he waved for the wineman to serve their table.

Cleve gestured for him to be seated.

"Is . . . your brother all right?" Tenna asked, a question she hadn't quite dared ask Lord Groghe.

Haligon's eyes twinkled with merriment. "You have taught him a lesson, too, you know."

"I don't usually go around knocking people down," Tenna began, and received another surreptitious jab in her ribs from Rosa, sitting beside her. "Except when they need it." She leaned forward, away from Rosa. "I meant to hit *you*."

Haligon rubbed his jaw. "I'm as glad enough you didn't. When Master Torlo told me that you'd been kept from running for three days, I knew I was very much at fault. Then he told me of the other near-misses. Will you accept this leather in compensation, with my apology?"

"Your father has already apologized."

"I make my own, Runner Tenna," he said with an edge to his voice and a solemn expression.

"I accept, but..." She was about to refuse the leather when, once again, Rosa jabbed her. She'd have sore ribs at this rate. "I accept."

"Good, for I should have a miserable Gather without your forgiveness," Haligon said, his expression lightening. Lifting the glass he had just been served, he tilted it in her direction and drank. "Will you save me a dance?"

Tenna pretended to consider. But she was secretly thrilled, for despite their first encounter, there was something about Haligon that she found very attractive. Just in case, she shifted in her chair, moving her upper body away from Rosa to avoid another peremptory jab.

"I was hoping to be able to do the toss dance," she began and, when Haligon eagerly opened his mouth to claim that, she added, "but my right leg isn't entirely sound."

"But sound enough surely for the quieter dances?" Haligon asked. "You seemed to be walking well enough."

"Yes, walking's no strain for me . . ." and Tenna hesitated a little longer, "but I would enjoy having a partner." Which allowed him to ask for more than one dance.

"The slow ones, then?"

"Beveny asked for one, remember," Rosa said casually.

"When does the dancing start?" Tenna asked.

"Not until full dark, after the meal," Haligon said. "Would you be my supper partner?"

She heard Rosa inhale sharply but she really did find him an agreeable sort. Certainly the invitation was acceptable. "I would be delighted to," she said graciously.

It was so arranged and Haligon toasted the agreement with the last of his wine, rose, bowed to them all, and left the table.

"Yo-ho, Tenna," Rosa murmured as they watched his tall figure disappear in the Gather crowd.

Cleve, too, grinned. "Neatly done. Do hope you'll be back on another Cross soon in case we have some more problems you can help us with."

"Oh, run off, will you?" Tenna replied flippantly.

Now she allowed herself to finger the dark green leather hide. "Was he watching us, do you suppose? How'd he know?"

"Oh, no one's ever said Haligon was a dimwit," Rosa said. "Though he is, riding runner traces like he has."

"*He* must have told his father, then," Cleve said. "Owning up to all that shows an honest nature. I might end up liking him after all."

"Proper order," Rosa said. "Though he never admitted using the traces before when Torlo braced him on that." She grinned at Tenna. "It's sure true that a pretty girl gets more attention than a plain one like me."

"You are not plain," Cleve said indignantly and realized he had fallen into Rosa's neatly laid trap to elicit a compliment from him.

"I'm not?" she replied, smiling archly.

"Oh, you!" he said with the wordless disgust of the well-baited. Then he laughed and carefully split Groghe's glass between their glasses. "Much too good to waste."

Tenna returned to the station long enough to put away the beautiful leather. And long enough to get many requests for dances and to be supper partner from other runners who congratulated her.

"Told ya so, dinnit I?" Penda said, catching Tenna's arm as she was leaving. The woman was grinning from ear to ear. "Pretty girl's always heard, ya know."

Tenna laughed. "And Haligon's going to stay off the traces."

"So his father promised," Penda said, "but we'll have to see does he."

"I'll see that he does," Tenna promised airily and returned to the Gather Square. She'd never had such a marvelous time before.

The supper lines were now forming down the road at the roasting pits and she began to wonder if Haligon had just been funning her and had never intended, Lord Holder's son that he was, to honor his invitation. Then he appeared beside her, offering his arm.

"I didn't forget," he murmured, taking her by the arm.

Being partnered with a Holder's son allowed them to patronize a different line at the roasting pits and so they were served well before Cleve and Rosa. The wine Haligon ordered was more of the excellent one she'd sampled in the afternoon so Tenna was quite merry and relaxed by the time the dancing began.

What surprised her, because she'd given the first dance to Grolly—as much because he didn't expect to get any dances from such a pretty girl as because he asked her first—was that Haligon did not dance it with someone else. He waited at the table for a breathless Grolly to bring her back. It was a sprightly enough tune for dancing but not as fast or complicated as the toss was. The next dance was at a slower tempo and she held out her hand to Haligon, despite the fact that half the male runners at the Gather were now crowding about for a chance to dance with her.

He pulled her into his arms with a deft movement and they were suddenly cheek to cheek. He was only a little taller than she was so their steps matched effortlessly. One circuit of the room and she had perfect confidence in his leading.

Since they were dancing cheek to cheek—he was only a little taller than she was—she could feel his face muscles lifting in a smile. And he gave her a quick pressure with both hands.

"Do you know when you're running again?"

"I've already had a short leg, down to the port," she said. "Enough for a good warm-up."

"How *do* you manage such long distances on your own legs?" he asked, holding her out slightly to see her face in the light of the glowbaskets that lined the dance floor. He really wanted to know, too.

"Part of it's training, of course. Part that my Blood is bred to produce runners."

"Could you have done anything else with your life?"

"I could but I like running. There's a sort of... magic to it. Sometimes you feel you could run 'round the world. And I like night running. You feel like you're the only one awake and alive and moving."

"Quite likely you are, save for dimwits on mounts on traces they shouldn't be using," he said in a wry tone. "How long *have* you been running?"

He sounded genuinely interested. She had thought perhaps she had made a mistake, being sentimental about something as commonplace as running.

"Almost two whole Turns. This is my first Cross."

"And I was a dimglowed idiot who interrupted it," he said in an apologetic tone.

Tenna was almost embarrassed at his continued references to his mistake.

"How often do I have to say I've forgiven you?" she said, putting her lips closer to his ear. "That green leather is going to make fine shoes for me. By the way, how'd you know that was the hide I wanted? Were you following us about?"

"Father said I had to make amends in some way more personal than handing you marks . . ."

"You didn't give Tanner Ligand what he asked for, did you?" Her query was sharp, because she didn't want him to have had to spend more than she felt necessary. And she leaned away from his guiding arm enough so that she could see his face as he answered

"I won't tell you how much, Tenna, but we struck a fair bargain. Trouble was," and now Haligon's voice was rueful, "he knew just how much I needed that particular hide. It's the talk of the Gather, you know."

Tenna suspected that it was and she hoped she could tell it to her own station before they heard rumor, which always exaggerated.

"Hmmm. I should have expected that," she said. "I shall be able to make two pairs of summer shoes out of that much leather and I'll think of you every time I wear them." She grinned up at him.

"Fair enough." Evidently satisfied by this exchange, he resettled his arms about her, drawing her just that much closer. "You didn't seem as interested

TENNA

in any other hide, you know. So I'd got off more lightly than I thought I might. I didn't know runners made their own footwear."

"We do and it's much better to make them for yourself. Then you've only yourself to blame if you've blisters."

"Blisters? They would be bad for a runner."

"Almost as bad as sticklebush slivers."

He groaned. "Will I ever be able to live that down?"

"You can try." Maybe she could get him to dance with her all night. He was possibly the best partner she'd ever had. Not that she ever lacked for them. But he was subtly different. In his dancing, too, for he seemed to know many combinations of the dance steps and she really had to keep her attention on her feet and following his lead. Maybe it was him being a Holder's son.

"Maybe it's being a runner," and his remark startled her, it being near what she'd just been thinking, "but you're the lightest thing on your feet." He reset his hands more firmly about her, drawing her as close as he could.

They were both silent, each concentrating on the complexities of the dance. It ended all too soon for Tenna. She didn't really wish to release him. Nor he, her. So they stood on the dance floor, arms at their sides but not with much distance between them. The music began again, a faster dance, and before she could say a word, Haligon had swung her into his arms and moved off in the rhythm of this tune. This time they had to concentrate not only on the steps but also to avoid collisions with more erratic dancers whirling about the floor.

Three dances to a set and Haligon whisked her off the floor during the change of musicians on the pretext of needing a drink. With glasses of chilled white wine, he guided her into the shadow of a deserted stall.

She smiled to herself, rehearsing a number of deft rejections if she needed them.

"I don't think you're at all lame, Tenna," he said conversationally. "Especially if the station master let you take a run down to the port. Care to have a go at the first toss dance after all?"

His expression dared her.

"We'll see."

Pause.

"So, will you run on tomorrow?"

"I'll be careful with the wine in case I do," she said, half warning him as she lifted the glass.

"Will you make it to the sea from here in one run?"

"Quite likely. It's spring and there'd be no snow on the pass trace."

"Would you still go if there were?"

"No one said anything about snow on the pass trace at the station."

"Keep your ears open, won't you?"

"A runner always needs to know conditions on the trace." She gave him a stern look.

"All right, I've got the message."

"Fair enough."

Pause.

"You're not at all what I expected, you know," Haligon said respectfully.

"I can quite candidly say the same of you, Haligon," she replied.

The new musicians played the first bar of the next song, to acquaint people with a sample of the dance to come.

So, when Tenna felt his arm about her shoulders, she did not resist the pressure. Nor did she when both arms enfolded her and his mouth found hers. It was a nice kiss, not sloppy as others had been, but well placed on her lips, as if he knew what he was about in kissing. His arms about her were sure, too, not crushing her needlessly against him. Respectful, she thought . . . and then, as the kiss deepened with her cooperation, she didn't think of anything but enjoying the experience.

Haligon monopolized her all evening, rather deftly, she realized. Always whisking her off the dance floor before anyone else could find her. They kissed quite a bit between dances. He was far more respectful of her person than she expected. And said so.

"With the punch you can deliver, my girl," he answered, "you can bet your last mark I'm not about to risk my brother's fate."

He also found other chilled drinks for her to drink instead of more wine. She appreciated that even more. Especially when the music of the toss dance began. The floor cleared of all save a few hardy couples.

"Shall we?" and Haligon's grin was all the challenge she needed.

The ache in her right shin was really minor and her confidence in his partnering had grown throughout the evening; otherwise she would not have taken his dare.

During the pattern of the dance, the female partner was to be swung as high as possible, and if she was very clever, she would twirl in midair before being caught by the male. It would be a dangerous dance, but it was ever so much fun. Tenna's older brother had taught her and given her enough practice so that she was well able to make the turns. It had ensured her partners at any Gather in the east once it was known how light she was and what a good dancer.

From the very first toss, she knew that Haligon was the best partner she'd ever had. There was great cheering for them when she managed a full two turns in the air before he caught her. In one of the rare close movements of the dance, he whispered swift instructions so that she was prepared for the final toss. And able to execute it, sure he would be there to keep her from crashing on the floor. She was close enough to being missed so that the spectators gasped just as he caught her half a handspan above the floor. Another girl was not so lucky but suffered no more than the indignity of the fall.

Cleve, Rosa, Spacia, Grolly, and most of the station crowded about them when they left the dance floor, congratulating them on such a performance.

They were offered drinks, meat rolls, and other delicacies.

"Upholding the honor of the station," Cleve loudly proclaimed. "And the Hold, of course," he magnanimously added, bowing to Haligon.

"Tenna's the best partner I've ever had," Haligon replied sincerely, mopping his face.

Then Torlo reached through the crowd and tapped Tenna's shoulder.

"You're on the run list, Tenna," he said, emphasizing the warning with a nod.

"To the coast?"

"Aye, as you wished." Torlo gave Haligon a severe look.

"I'll escort you to the station, then, Tenna?" Haligon asked.

The harpers had struck up another slow dance. Rosa and Spacia were looking intensely at Tenna but she couldn't interpret their glances. She also knew her duty as a runner.

"This is the last dance then." And she took Haligon by the arm and led him to the floor.

Haligon tucked her in against him and she let her body relax against his and to his leading. She had never had such a Gather in her life. She could almost be glad that he'd run her off the trace and so started the events that had culminated in this lovely night.

They said nothing, both enjoying the flow of the dance and the sweet music. When it ended, Haligon led her from the floor, holding her right hand in his, and toward the station, its glowbasket shining at the door.

"So, Runner Tenna, you finish your first Cross. It won't be your last, will it?" Haligon asked as they paused just beyond the circle of light. He lifted his hand and lightly brushed back the curls.

"No, it's unlikely to. I'm going to run as long as I'm able."

"But you'll be Crossing often, won't you?" he asked, and she nodded. "So, if sometime in the future, when I've got my own holding . . . I'm going to breed runners . . . beasts, that is," he qualified hastily, and she almost laughed at his urgent correction. "I've been trying to find the strain I want to breed, you see, and used the traces as sort of the best footing for comparison. I mean, is there any chance you might . . . possibly . . . consider running more often on this side of the world?"

Tenna cocked her head at him, surprised by the intensity and roughness in his pleasant voice.

"I might." She smiled up at him. This Haligon

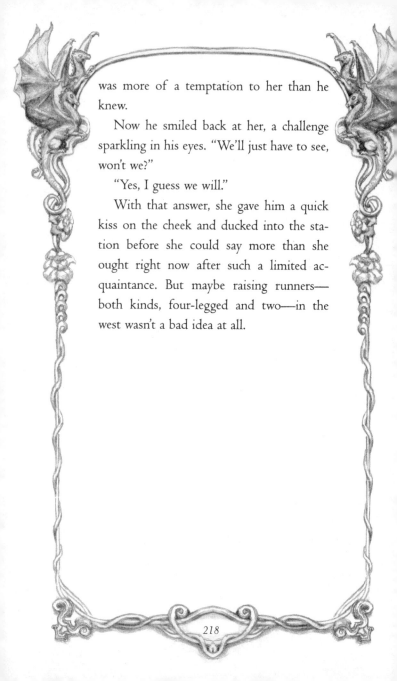

was more of a temptation to her than he knew.

Now he smiled back at her, a challenge sparkling in his eyes. "We'll just have to see, won't we?"

"Yes, I guess we will."

With that answer, she gave him a quick kiss on the cheek and ducked into the station before she could say more than she ought right now after such a limited acquaintance. But maybe raising runners—both kinds, four-legged and two—in the west wasn't a bad idea at all.

EVER
THE
TWAIN

*R*u was tired from helping his father load the fishing nets they had repaired the previous night, so he was lagging a bit behind his sister when a fresh breeze came up and stung him in the face. Immediately he was back on his dragon, at altitude above Ista Island—high enough to see the silvery haze on the horizon that marked the incoming fall of Thread.

That's the leading edge, Nerith, he told his dragon telepathically, as he checked that his safety straps were secure on the broad belt all dragonriders wore during Threadfall. The clump of Thread had been overlooked by the other riders in his Wing and Neru knew no one else would be able to sear it before the silvery Threads fell to the ground and devoured every living thing in their path.

Fly faster, Nerith! Neru urged his lifelong partner, his beloved dragon. *We must climb up higher and try to sear it as we draw near.*

I will reach it; my wings are strong, Nerith replied, and his wings beat down sending them higher and faster than they'd ever flown before. As they closed in on the leading edge of Thread, Nerith belched a long steady stream of flame, charring the silvery clump to harmless ash.

Scanning the skies around them closely, Neru saw one single long Thread that had escaped Nerith's flame. *Wheel and spin, Nerith, we've missed one!*

I see it! his dragon replied.

Abruptly, Nerith dropped his right wing to make the turn, and with one powerful stroke, he pivoted into position to flame the lone strand of Thread with a burst of fire. It was a very dangerous maneuver, but nothing Neru and Nerith hadn't done before.

You are the strongest, wisest, and fastest dragon on Pern, Nerith. Good flying, my friend. Well done! Neru said, as he caressed the soft hide of his dragon's neck.

Nerith turned his head toward Neru, his many-faceted eyes whirling blue with pride.

"Here comes the Ninny and her wannabe dragonrider brother," a baritone voice said nearby, cracking in adolescent fashion. Suddenly Neru was back in the present, on the road to the Harper's hall, and out of his

NERU
&
NIAN

daydream. Mostly the kids at Lado Hold on Ista Island called him Ru and his sister Ninny. Neru didn't mind "Ru," but he took extravagant exception whenever he heard people call his twin sister, Nian, by that nickname.

"Flamel, do you want yet another bloody nose?" Neru asked, as he focused on Flamel, son of the Hold's smith. Nian, who was very self-conscious and hated confrontation of any sort, moved slightly behind her twin brother.

"Sure," Flamel said, putting up his hands. But just then Orla, daughter of the Hold's weaver, intervened.

"You really are tiresome, Flamel. Just drop it for the day, huh? Give us all a break," she said in a cajoling tone of voice.

"Why should I? It's fun," Flamel said, raising his fists again. "Let's see how the dragonrider defends himself and his ninny of a sister."

"Oh, that's so old, Flamel. Can't you strive to be just a little creative?" Orla said with a bored sigh.

Just then two adults strode onto the road, talking together in low voices. The taller man glanced at the scene, then paused.

"You all better hurry on to the Harper's now, or you'll be late," he said with a flick of his hand. But as he passed he gave Flamel a hard stare. It was enough for the bully to move on, while Orla took her place beside Nian.

"Thanks, Orla," Neru said with one of his charming smiles. "And you're right. Flamel is boring."

"Just so long as you don't let him get to you again. Master Lado was not best pleased over your last fight with Flamel."

"But he didn't do anything to stop Flamel bullying my sister," Ru commented sourly.

" 'Childish bickering,' he called it," Nian said.

"When Flamel's apprenticed, it'll be knocked out of him," Orla replied tartly. "Oh, if it would only happen *soon*."

The three friends continued on their way down the road that led to the Harper's Hall and their morning lessons.

"Soon all of us will have to move on," Orla said, kicking a pebble out of the way. Her curly hair bounced with every step she took. "How will you manage being apart?" she asked Nian.

"Nian's tougher than she looks, Orla," Ru said, his twin's champion and supporter.

If only that were true, Nian thought. She was scared of the mere idea of being alone, day in and day out. She knew she would have to stand on her own two feet one day, but the thought of doing it without her other half nearby was frightening.

Being the more reserved twin, she couldn't imagine life without her brother at her side, even if she could always sense him. When her parents had moved Neru to a bedroom in the lean-to, she had spent many wakeful nights without his comforting presence beside her, even though she was well aware that boys and girls were always separated when they got to a certain age. But being in totally different places . . . She gave herself a mental shake. It would do no good to worry now.

"Has Master Ruart recommended you to the Healer and Harper Halls?" Orla asked. "I get to go to Fort Hold, as apprentice to Master Elaine. But not until the leaves turn. Master Elaine designed that gorgeous brocade pattern our family's working on right now."

"Father wants to marry Nian off to a farmer on the North Shore," Neru said with some perturbation. He glanced at his sister to see her reaction.

She shrugged. Her mother had been making remarks lately about how good it was to start a new life in one's own place, but Nian tried not to listen.

"We're keeping an eye open for fire lizard clutches," she said. "So we can be apart without really being separated." The fire lizards, distant cousins to the much larger dragons, were good companions and useful for delivering messages. It had been Neru's idea that if they both had fire lizards, they would at least be able to communicate with each other over distance, thus making their imminent physical separation more bearable.

"How soon will Clidith's clutch be ready for Impression?" Orla asked. "This could be your big chance, Ru."

"First I have to be Searched, you know," Ru said with a diffident shrug.

"Don't try to fool me, Ru," Orla said firmly. "Not that every lad doesn't hope to be a dragonrider. I think you'd make a good one. Especially since you are so good a brother. *And* I hear that one of the eggs is a queen egg." She turned excitedly to Nian. "You could become a dragonrider, too, Nian!"

"Who would want a Ninny for a rider?" Nian asked scornfully.

"You shouldn't call yourself that, Ni," Ru said with a fierce scowl. "A ninny you're not. Don't even think it of yourself."

Nian glanced gratefully at her brother.

"You can't let the teasing of a dimwit like Flamel get to you," Orla said with equal severity. "As we used to say, 'Sticks and stones may break your bones, but names can never hurt you.'"

Nian gave a snort and wished she could shake off such jibes as easily, but she didn't have that kind of confidence. No one ever teased Orla. Orla was self-assured and pretty, with very curly black hair that framed her oval face. Her nose was straight and small, her mouth wide and friendly. Orla had all the feminine qualities that Nian did not see in herself. She didn't consider herself even marginally attractive.

While Nian, Neru, and Orla had been strolling in a leisurely way as they talked, the rest of the children of Lado Hold were making their way down the hill toward the Harper's small Hall. Their nemesis, Flamel, tall for his age yet still carrying some baby flab, was visible in the group. He immediately edged closer to the twins to begin teasing.

"You been Searched yet, Ru?" was Flamel's snide query. Singling out her brother was unfair, anyway, Nian thought, because so many of the other boys in the Hold desperately wished to become dragonriders and escape the less glamorous adult occupations waiting for them. But Neru's dream was well known, and she thought that Flamel chose his targets carefully, knowing exactly how to insult and injure.

Ru ignored the question and Nian was proud of him. Her mother had constantly told them to ignore such taunts.

"Well, you're still here, aren't you. Neru? We're all waiting for the dragons to come take you away."

Neru shook his shoulders as if he could dislodge the verbal darts sent his way. But Nian was provoked into angry responses.

"He will be Searched, you just wait and see!" Nian brandished her fist at the flabby son of the Journeyman Smith, who merely snorted at her. "They sure won't give you even a sniff, Flamel."

"You scare me," Flamel said, pretending to quiver and knocking his knees together.

"Stop it, Flamel," said Orla. "You really are pathetic, you know. Leave the twins alone. Just for a change."

"Or?" Flamel replied.

"Or I might just tell everyone here the real reasons why you pick on the twins so much. I might just tell them all that you're really—"

"Really what?" Flamel interrupted her quickly. Orla was not the only one to notice that the color in his cheeks was rising to a pinkish blush.

"Shall we see?" Orla asked in her sweetest tone.

Flamel gave her a long stare, but he began to walk faster, putting distance between him and Orla, as well as Nian and Neru. Nian smiled her thanks at Orla, who sketched an airy salute.

"My pleasure. He gives me a headache with his nonsense. I hope his father does send him to the Smithhold at Telgar. They'll sort him out soon enough."

That reminded Nian—again—all too forcefully that there were changes in the air for all the youngsters in their age group. She didn't like her father's talk of marrying her to a farmer on the north coast of Ista. She had met the man at Gathers, and she was not overjoyed by the thought of closer ties. Nothing had been said about Neru, though she knew that her parents had decided a long time ago that he was to be trained at something other than fishing. There were quite enough in that profession already at Lado Hold, and Neru had shown no aptitude for a life at sea. Their mother wanted the Harper, Ruart, to recommend Neru for harper training, since he performed very well on the flute and the horn. His voice had changed into a good enough tenor range that he was always asked to sing at Gathers.

The children had reached the lean-to porch of the Harper's so-called Hall and were all busy scraping mud off their boots. They would not bring any mud into the Hall and have to clean it up later. Ruart insisted on high standards of tidiness. The porch, which was broad enough to accommodate the Hold's children during fair weather, was their favorite place for lessons, but as today was raw and cold, with a clammy mist in the air, they'd have to remain inside.

Inside, the "Hall" had been enlarged from the original limestone cave. A ledge against one wall provided a bench, all too often as cold as the rock behind it, for the smaller children to sit on. Another alcove was Harper Ruart's private quarters, screened from the main room by one of Orla's beautiful screens, its panels woven of fragrant reeds and grasses, which still faintly scented the stone room. The screen also doubled as a wall on which to hang the drawings of Ruart's students. Everyone in Lado Hold was certain that Orla was going to be a fine artist—probably the only one ever to go forward from Lado to an Artist's Hall. Her skillful drawings stood out vividly, compared to the scrawls and scenes by the other students.

The youngest children sat on their ledge; niches

had been carved out below the seating to shelve their books and slates. Two fine wooden tables allowed the older students a proper surface for writing and figuring. Ruart had a splendid desk made of the local woods, with a series of drawers on each side in which he kept records and texts that were rare, and thus too valuable to be left out. Behind him, a slab of black slate had been cleverly attached to the smoothest part of the limestone wall. On this he could write and display whatever the day's lessons might be.

At sixteen Turns old and soon to be apprenticed to learn a trade, Neru, Nian, Orla, Flamel, and Chaum were the oldest, if not the most advanced, students. Journeyman Ruart had high hopes for the twins and Orla, but the other two boys would undoubtedly perfect adult skills in the plantations and fields that surrounded Lado Hold.

The journeyman harper was about to take the roll call when wild shrieks and yells interrupted.

"Dragons, dragons!"

Journeyman Ruart was as startled as his class. Someone pounded up the steps and rapped on his door, shouting urgently.

"The dragons come on Search!"

The room erupted with noise as the children jostled for the door and a closer look at the magnificent dragons. Almost every child on Pern, at one time or another, dreamed of flying a-dragonback.

Ruart clapped his hands together and shouted at the children. "Settle! Settle now, children! You'll all be allowed out to see the dragons on Search, but not a one of you will do so in an unfitting manner!" He lowered his voice when this threat had the desired effect.

"Of course, you all know that there is an age requirement for being Searched," he continued slowly and deliberately. "You little ones will have to stay at the back." His hands made a shooing gesture. "Now let us all proceed outside in a quiet and orderly fashion. No pushing."

Two green dragons and one beautifully sea-blue dragon had fitted themselves on Lado's little Gather clearing in front of the main Hold. Lord Lado and his lady, Cirine, hastily smoothing her apron, were already outside to greet the arrivals. Ruart skillfully motioned his class to form ranks across the roadway.

"We come on Search," the blue rider said formally, dismounting with an athletic grace that Neru admired. Nian glanced nervously at her twin. Would his dream come true today? Would he be Searched by the dragons? Was this the last she'd see of her "other half" until who knew when?

"I am R'dik, blue Shalanth's rider, and here are Sarty, green Ledith's rider and Conna, who rides Oswith."

Beside her Ru shuffled his feet, swung his arms, and all but nominated himself out of hand as a candidate. She pinched his sleeve to remind him of his manners. Giving her a cross look, he nevertheless subsided. Just as he protected her against physical danger, she protected him from making social errors.

"Search, and be welcome, R'dik," Lord Lado replied, equally formally. "The youngsters of our Hold are all available to you and your dragons." He gestured to those ranked in front of him, all breathless with suspense. "The Hold is greatly honored by your Search. I hear that Clidith clutched thirty-two eggs."

"Yes. They are near to being Hatched, and we would like to provide the Weyr with plenty of choices," he said, with a bow that swept from Lado around to the children, who bowed back. He smiled encouragingly at them. "We are looking for those who are fourteen Turns or older," he announced. "For, as you all know, we are in a Pass and need to have riders who are fit and able to join the fighting wings as soon as the hatchlings grow strong enough to fly."

Ruart adroitly directed his disappointed younger students to sit out of the way, on the Hold steps, while the older ones ranked beside him to brave the Search. While he thought Chaum might make a good, if unimaginative, rider, he devoutly hoped that the bullying Flamel, who had straightened up as if he was certain of being chosen, would be totally ignored. Neru, he knew, wanted desperately to be a dragonrider; perhaps both twins might be selected. Ruart had never heard of twins being made riders at the same Hatching, but oh, how that would solve the problem of separating Neru and Nian! He caught a glimpse of Palla, the twins' mother, among the crowd now assembling outside the Hold to watch the dragons on Search. Her youngest child, Niall, was in her arms, waving at his older brother and sister.

After a thorough inspection of the waiting teenagers, Ledith and Oswith picked Orla and Chaum out of the crowd. Then they approached Nian, sniffing at her and giving her little prods with their noses. She was made a little nervous by this close inspection, and she grabbed her brother's hand. The dragons didn't seem one bit interested in Neru.

Nian heard her mother gasp as she, too, saw the dragons overlook her eager, would-be dragonrider son.

How could this be happening? Neru thought of nothing but dragons and fighting Thread. How could they overlook him and show such interest in her, when Nian had never once entertained the thought of dragons except for her brother's sake? This is a bad situation, she thought. If they take me on Search and leave Ru behind, I'll have deserted him and stolen his dream all in the same moment. I can't let this happen!

Unconsciously Nian shifted her weight toward her brother, changing her stance from that of protected to protector. She had to make them take Ru with her—but how?

The green dragon, Ledith, turned to Oswith as if in consultation. Then Conna stepped to her dragon as if summoned to her side.

She is very strong! Oswith told her rider. *I can hear her, Conna. But she will not go without him.*

Remaining at Oswith's side, Conna looked at the twins. "What is your name?" she asked Nian.

"Neru and Nian," the twins chorused in unison.

"It's certainly unanimous," the blue rider said, a wide smile on his tanned face. He slapped his riding gauntlets against his thigh. "Ah, I see that you are twins."

"Yes, blue rider, we are, though my sister is the elder," Neru said as Nian still gripped his hand tightly. By the First Egg! Neru hoped that the dragons would select him, too. But what if it *were* Nian, not he, Neru, who was taken on Search? What if he never had the chance to fulfill his dream? He simply couldn't—wouldn't—think about it. Neru decided that his best plan was no plan at all. He'd just have to wait and see what happened to him.

"Have you ever been separated from each other?" Sarty asked, startling everyone.

"No, rider Sarty," Neru replied.

"We're just better together at everything," Nian added stoutly.

Which, as the holders and Ruart knew, was true enough.

Conna gave a little sniff. "Well, we'll see what the dragons decide," she said. "Are your parents here?"

"I am their mother, Palla. Their father has not yet returned from the morning's fishing," Palla said, moving through the crowd toward the dragonriders and the possible candidates.

"It is customary to seek the permission of the

Holder and at least one parent of any Searched candidate," Conna said, turning expectantly to Lado. "The dragons have chosen Nian."

"But my son has shown more interest in becoming a dragonrider, while Nian never has. How can such a choice be made?"

"It sometimes happens. The green dragons *know* these things and, despite riding Oswith nearly thirty Turns now, I have never figured out how she discerns rider potential."

"But they would be separated so soon, too soon!" said Palla, tears starting to form in her eyes.

"Oh, Mother," Neru mumbled in embarrassed exasperation, hoping that only his twin heard him. Nian squeezed his fingers.

"They would soon be separated anyway, would they not?" asked Conna kindly.

At that moment Nian made up her mind. She had never thought of being a dragonrider, but now that she had been Searched, and the possibility existed, she would certainly do her best to try and make her brother's dream come true.

"Em, pardon me, dragonriders," she squawked, and had to pause to clear the little frog that had crept up into her throat and made her croak. She continued.

"If I may? No one else from my family will be able to attend the Hatching and, should I Impress a dragon, I'd like to have a family member nearby. Could my brother not come with me now?" Squeezing Ru's hand tightly, she looked at the dragons and their riders beseechingly, and willed it to happen with all her might. Neru squeezed her hand back and held his breath. He knew that dragonriders' families were allowed to visit the Weyr, particularly on special occasions. But would they let him come now?

Conna paused a moment and looked at her dragon, lost in a telepathic conversation.

The boy is strong but his twin shields him from me, Oswith said to her rider. *I cannot see his potential clearly. It is strange. Perhaps he should come along as a candidate, too.*

"Oswith is undecided about Neru as a candidate, but we will bring him with us regardless," Conna said finally. Both twins let out their breath in a rush. "Never fear, Nian, your brother will remain with you until the Hatching. There is, however, no guarantee that any of those selected on Search will Impress; the hatchlings make that decision."

"Oh!" Palla clasped both her hands to her throat. "But the dragons seemed so interested in Nian." Her eyes were wide with concern.

Ledith seemed to sneeze. "We can never guarantee," Sarty repeated equably, "but Ledith is rarely wrong."

"Whichever," Holder Lado said brusquely. Kind as he was, he was not fond of long, drawn-out farewells. "Now, run along and pack what you need to take with you. Don't keep these dragonriders waiting—they may have other places to Search."

Looking pleased that Lado Hold could offer the Weyr four possible dragonriders, he flapped his hands at those selected—Neru and Nian, Orla and Chaum—to be off to their holds, and then gestured to Ruart to take his charges back to the Hall for their lessons. Then a holder woman appeared with hot mugs of klah and the best wineglasses full of a red that Lado had imported from Benden especially for such occasions.

The two women riders reached for the klah, but R'dik took a glass of wine and, sipping respectfully, made approving noises as he swallowed, nodding with appreciation to the Holder.

At their family hold, Palla stuffed clean underclothes and socks into a worn leather carryall for Neru and tossed Nian a canvas bag made from old sail, all the while protesting that they really had nothing suitable to be seen in a Weyr. Nian neatly folded her Gather dress, and Neru's fine Gather shirt, which she had embroidered for him, and reached for their worn winter jackets. Everyone knew that going *between* was very cold. She found her knitted cap, but not Ru's, and then saw the bobble of it extruding from one of his jacket pockets. They had only their heavy boots, since once the weather was warm enough, everyone on Ista Island usually went about barefoot. All too quickly they were ready and Palla hugged them both, tears streaming down her face.

"We're not going to our deaths, Mother," Neru said, embarrassed though there was only family to see her make such a display.

"Will you let me ride your dragon, Ni?" Niall asked his older sister.

"If I Impress I surely will," Nian replied kindly.

"Dragonriders are always very generous about giving rides, but not by yourself," Ru added.

They heard a most unusual sound outside, almost a growl. Niall ran to the window.

"There're two dragons waiting outside!" he announced excitedly.

Nian kissed her mother several times, carefully blotting the tears on her face. "We will be back, you know," she said. "It'd be no trouble at all to drop in any time we can." Though she was not at all sure

she'd be a dragonrider, she was determined to think positively. Especially about Ru. No matter how things turned out for her, Neru *must* Impress.

Palla followed them to the door, saw them being shown how to mount the green dragons, and ended up waving and weeping as the dragons flung themselves into the sky and disappeared with her children.

It was very cold, Nian thought, daring to press back against Conna for warmth.

"Don't be afraid, Nian," the dragonrider said in her ear. "Now, we are going *between*, so take a deep breath, and by the time you have counted to eight we will be back in the sunshine and circling over Ista Weyr. Ready? Start counting *now!*"

Between was cold; colder than anything Nian had ever experienced. It was also very dark *between*, which she should have remembered from the ballads Ruart had so diligently taught his students. The song came to her mind—"Black, blacker, blackest"—and then, just as Conna had said, they were suddenly warmed by the bright morning sun and circling down to land at Ista Weyr. The last time the twins had come for a Gather here, they had sailed in her father's boat. From above, Ista didn't look as big as Nian had remembered, but it was still bigger than Lado Hold.

There were people to welcome them and Nian tried to maintain her newly found confidence and *not* hide behind Ru who, as ever, spoke for both of them.

"I'm Kilpie, in charge of the Lower Caverns," announced an older, slightly stout lady whose sun-streaked blond hair was neatly braided and coiled around her head. She had a stern mouth, but her eyes were welcoming and alight with good humor.

"Come, I shall show you candidates where you will be staying. And you can meet the others whom the dragons have Searched for the Hatching. Which, I might add, won't be long now. Come along. When I've shown you around," she added, shooing them all in front of her, "you are to come back here for a snack. There's always something to eat for hungry riders. We keep klah, soup, or porridge warm all day and all night." She pointed to a small hearth at the far end of the cavern where, indeed, pots sat at the back, keeping warm. "And fresh bread when it's ready."

Ru grinned at his sister. He was always hungry,

now that he was growing tall and filling out his bones. Pretty soon he'd be taller than Nian.

The main kitchen cavern of Ista Weyr was immense, and some of the stalactites had been left in place as if holding up its stony roof. Along the outside wall, with chimneys built in to take cooking odors out of the huge room, were the hearths and ovens, just like the kitchen in Lado's much smaller hold. But here some of the hearths were enormous, and the heat they gave off would be intolerable in full summer, Nian thought. Would she and Neru both be there in full summer? Tables and chairs were placed around the main dining area, with a platform for the head table where the Weyrleaders would dine with guests. She hoped candidates were not considered "guests." Everyone would be looking at them, and Nian did not like to be the object of scrutiny. It made her conscious of herself and her plain looks.

Kilpie led them down a broad corridor and into another wide cavern. This was on two levels, a passage leading to curtained alcoves and steps down to a living area filled with comfortable chairs, tables, and storage chests. She pointed to the curtained passage that led to the baths and necessaries.

"And we expect everyone living in the Weyr to be clean for breakfast and dinner every day. Now, there will be empty sleeping alcoves along here, unless people have been changing about, but pick one that doesn't look occupied and you'll be all right if your bags are displayed. I've put a white candidate's robe in every alcove, so that you'll all have them to hand."

"Are there many of us candidates?" Orla asked.

"Forty, so far," Kilpie said. "And more coming in, as we have thirty-two eggs and wish to give the hatchlings ample choice."

"But how will we know when the Hatching starts?" Neru asked, wondering how quickly he could get his robe on and make it to the Hatching Ground on time. Thirty-two eggs and more than forty candidates to stand. Well, even if the dragons hadn't picked him outright, he would remain positive. He just *had* to Impress his very own dragon!

Kilpie regarded him a long moment. "The dragons begin to hum a welcome to the hatchlings. As soon as you hear them, drop everything and change into the white robe and present yourself at the Hatching Ground." She pointed to the opening at the far end of the living area. Crouching down a bit and looking in that direction, Nian could see the great arch of the Hatching Ground entrance directly across the Bowl of Ista Weyr. "There will also be a lot of coming and going as guests are brought in.

And your parents, if they have chosen to come to the Hatching." She made a noise halfway between a snort and a sigh. "So, go along now," she said, gesturing to the alcoves, "and settle yourselves in. Then come back to the main cavern. I believe there're sweet buns and cool fruit juice or klah waiting for you."

The promise of food had the newly selected candidates immediately rushing toward the curtains, peeking past them to find the untaken alcoves.

Neru and Nian, with an unspoken thought, moved to the far end and chose alcoves side by side. Orla and Chaum followed their lead; Orla's eyes were bright with curiosity, and Chaum, who was rarely excited by anything, still kept close to those he knew.

Nian's alcove included a bed, a chest, and several pegs on the wall. The white candidate's robe hung on one of the pegs. She held it up against her. The straight lines would fit anyone, covering all but the tallest to the knees, and the sleeves were not too long. The fabric was very soft from much use and careful laundering, and Nian wondered how many successful candidates had worn this particular robe over the Turns. Would their luck rub off on her and Neru, too?

Just then Neru entered her sleeping alcove. "You can't have unpacked already," she accused him.

"No, I put my carryall smack in the middle of

the bed so anyone would see that the room is occupied. But I'm hungry and could sure use some sweet buns to tide me over until supper." He picked her carryall up where she had dropped it to the floor and plopped it on her bed. "I'm going to look silly wearing something like that. It's nearly a dress."

"It's a candidate's robe, and who would ever have expected this morning that we'd be chosen to wear one?"

"Not me," her twin said staunchly.

"And the same back at you, Ru."

"They were smart to pick Chaum and Orla, too," her brother said, pleased.

She heard his stomach growling and grinned at him. She carefully hung the robe back on its peg. "Let's go eat."

No one was late for the snack, Kilpie remarked when the lot of them arrived back to the kitchen cavern and took seats at the table she designated. The juice was cool and tart, while the sweet breads were dotted with nuts and dried berries and were so tender that Nian and Neru hoped there'd be more than one apiece. They were joined by a white-haired older man who introduced himself as H'ran, Weyrlingmaster, rider of bronze Prinith. He looked them over one by one and smiled.

"Now, I've a few words of advice for you candidates. First, the new hatchling is invariably starving. There will be bowls of meat for you to feed him or her to the stuffing point. Hatchlings can be a little unnerving as they stagger around looking for their riders, so don't be surprised or fearful of such antics and be quick on your feet to get out of their way. If you're the one they want to Impress, you'll know it."

"How?" asked a very pretty girl who was dressed in the finest blue robe Nian had ever seen.

"That dress of hers was expensive," Orla murmured in Nian's ear. "That blue dye is hard to get." Orla knew about such things.

"How?" H'ran grinned. It was an unexpectedly soft and loving expression, which Nian thought remarkable in an older man. "It's unmistakable. You'll immediately know their name. Added to that, they act as if they owned you, keeping any other hatchling from getting near you. They may be wet-winged and newly hatched, but they can move fairly fast once they've discovered their rider. Watch out for their claws. They're sharp and dangerous, even if they don't mean to hurt anyone. They're as anxious to Impress as you are to be Impressed. But don't worry. The Weyrleaders and I will be on the Hatching Ground with you to organize the stampede. And there'll be plenty of food to stuff their guts. Bring any questions you have about your hatchling to me. That's what me and Prinith are here for."

If anyone had questions, they weren't bold enough to voice them and so, when all the sweet breads were eaten, H'ran suggested that they follow him to the weyrling barracks so they'd know which direction to take with their dragons when Impression had been made. The barracks were exactly that—not nearly as homey or comfortable as the alcoves. There was a broad wooden bed for the hatchling, well marked by generations of dragon claws, and above it, a narrow shelf with bedding on it for the rider.

"Once you get your dragon settled here, you can return to the main living quarters if you wish. It's up to yourselves." The way he said it gave Nian the feeling that all new riders chose to stay with their dragons. Well, if Ru were here, she'd want to be, too. That is, if they both Impressed. "You'll always know if your dragon needs you, I promise you that much," H'ran added, and brushed his thick hair back in a nervous gesture.

"Now, if you'll follow me across the Bowl, I'll show you the eggs."

Dutifully, but with murmurs of excitement, they followed him through the arches onto the Hatching

Ground. In groups of two or three, the eggs reposed on the warm sands. Nian was glad she had on heavy boots, because those with lighter footwear were obviously feeling the heat, imitating the stalk of river birds searching shallow waters for tiny edibles.

"It's called the Hatching dance," H'ran said, trying to keep his face solemn as he also stepped quickly and carefully. "Move among the eggs, if you wish. They're not quite hard enough, but will be very soon. Getting used to them in advance seems to help when the moment comes."

"Can we touch them?" Chaum asked.

"Never known it to do any harm," H'ran said indulgently. Chaum instantly stretched his hand out and touched the egg he was standing by. And yanked his fingers away.

"It should feel warm," H'ran said, shifting his sandaled feet more quickly now. "Go on. I'll be right outside," he added, and made his way back to the main arch.

Tugging Nian by the hand, Neru trotted over to the nearest eggs with his sister in tow. One, the biggest one Nian was sure, lay just beyond on a slight rise. It had light tan mottles on its golden shell and Nian thought it was the prettiest of the eggs. Neru hauled her to the one he fancied, with mottles of a slightly darker tan. Boldly he ran both hands over the top of the shell. "It is warm, Nian, just feel it."

"I like that one," she said, pointing, and broke his grasp to go examine her pretty egg more closely. "It's the biggest one, too. Could it be the queen?"

"Hmmm, possibly, Ni," he allowed, but he was more interested in his egg than hers.

"D'you think they can tell which color the dragon will be from its shell?" Nian asked pensively, running her hand along the widest part of the egg. Nearby, Orla was investigating another egg, while Chaum still stood apart, surveying the entire clutch. The very pretty girl in blue sauntered over toward Nian, a stern expression on her face, as if warning Nian away from her chosen egg. Nian gave her a quick glance and moved away to join Orla.

"She's the Masterfarmer's daughter, and her name is Robina," Orla said softly to Nian. "She told us—" Orla paused to wink at Nian. "—that she's been promised the queen egg."

"You heard what the Searchers said. No one can guarantee Impression. It's up to the hatchlings."

"Well, you'd make a much better queen rider than that snotty stuck-up old wherry."

"It's not me that must Impress. It's Neru," Nian said firmly.

"It's still up to the hatchlings," Orla repeated.

The two girls wandered over to Neru, who was reciting to some others what he knew about dragons. Nian realized her twin was not happy that he had been a final addition to those Searched. Knowing that he tended to keep his feelings to himself, Nian peered at him intently and reached for the connection she always felt with him. He most certainly was putting up a brave front, and she wondered how long he would be able to maintain it. Nian knew, without a shadow of a doubt, that her twin would be gutted if she Impressed a dragon and he did not. She wished she could find the words to reassure him.

"There're some who think they can predict colors, but from what I've heard, no one ever gets all the colors right in a Hatching from just looking at the shell," Neru said. His glance followed the pretty girl who was now circling Nian's egg. "Except maybe the queen," he added.

"Well, this shell is sort of bronzy. Maybe you'd better make up to it, too," Nian said with a little laugh. "You have to be a bronze rider."

He gave a shrug and looked around him. "I think you're right about yours being bigger than any of the others," he told her. "But if it's the queen, it won't help me." And he continued to stroke his chosen egg.

From the entrance, H'ran gestured with his arm to gather them all together. "All right now, candidates, we have some evening chores we could use some help with."

The word "chores" evoked a groan from some candidates, but everyone followed H'ran as he led them into another cavern where five dragons lay, their wings or other parts of their bodies covered with towels of some sort. There was a flooring of fine, warm sand—not as hot as the Hatching Ground, but comfortable for the dragons as a bed.

"Not the nicest of jobs, but you will have to learn how to tend your own dragons, so you might as well start today. These were casualties in the last Threadfall, two days ago." Neru thought of his morning's daydream and then paid close attention to what H'ran was saying. "We soothed their wounds with numbweed, and right now the compresses have to be changed. Ah, here come their riders.

"You can assist them in the task and gain some experience in the bargain. Being a dragonrider is not just about being able to fly anywhere you want to." H'ran gestured to several of the candidates to go to certain dragons, and although Neru and Nian would have been separated, she tagged after her brother as he was signaled to the bronze whose neck was festooned with towels.

"I'm C'tic," the bronze rider said amiably, "and poor old Brith here got badly tangled up in a clump of Thread." He began carefully peeling off the first towel.

"What's your name?" he asked, glancing up at Neru, and the twins replied in unison as they usually did.

"Well, then, Neru, get a towel, dunk it in the numbweed keg over there, wring it out, but not too thoroughly, and bring it over here."

While Brith had lowered his head and neck to permit the dressing, Nian saw the skin quivering as C'tic carefully inserted a fingernail under the towel and began to roll it back, revealing such raw-looking flesh that Nian shivered at the sight of it.

"Poor brave Brith," she said in the croon she used when one of her siblings suffered injuries.

"He's sure he's hurting much more than he really is," C'tic said amiably, beginning to loosen another towel. Neru carefully held a damp towel out by its corners, trying to hold his breath from the acrid smell of the numbweed-soaked fabric.

C'tic chuckled. "You get used to the smell of numbweed quickly," he said, taking the corners of the towel from Neru. Keeping it carefully stretched, he placed it flat on the raw-looking flesh. Brith gave a moan that was more relief at the coolness of the potion than pain.

"How long does it take him to heal?" Nian asked.

"Actually, they heal very quickly," C'tic replied. "You can see here on the shallower parts of the burn when the new skin is already forming after just a few days. Are you really interested?"

"Oh yes," Nian said.

"My sister is good at nursing," Neru said, staunchly.

"Well, if you aren't upset by such things, you can peel off that next towel while your brother gets a replacement. Easy now."

He watched her as she carefully slid her long index finger nail under the edge of the towel and began rolling it back as she had seen him do. He nodded approval. Brith's neck flesh quivered briefly, and then Ru was holding out a replacement dressing. Nian managed to get it neatly into place.

"Couldn't have done it better myself," C'tic said. "Hey, Brith, this is going to be a snap today," he said encouragingly to his dragon.

To one side of the infirmary, one of the other riders exclaimed in dismay, "Shards. We've got another fainter. Someone get me a cold compress while I brush all the sand off her; she certainly hit the dirt with a bang!"

Neru peered around those gathered to assist the fainter and he chuckled. "It's the girl in blue, Ni," he said with a little smirk. "The one who fancied your egg."

"There's usually one who's not good with wounds," C'tic said. "Has someone brought the restorative? That one will make a fine rider!" His tone was sarcastic.

"You'd think she'd be used to injured animals, being the Masterfarmer's daughter," Nian murmured to her brother.

"Now, she can't help the way she is," Neru said with considerably more charity than his sister expressed, "even if she *was* promised the gold."

"I'd pity the gold," Nian replied.

Brith carefully turned his head back to eye Nian and Neru. The blue of his faceted eyes was shot through with orange.

"We're not hurting you, are we?" Ru asked apologetically.

No. The twins gasped as the dragon's mind seemed to fill theirs. *The fresh numbweed is so soothing.*

"Did I really truly hear him speaking to me?" Ru

asked C'tic, who grinned at them. The question Nian sensed in her brother was that, to him, being bespoken by a dragon meant that he had a right to be a candidate.

"Dragons speak to anyone they want to," C'tic said, reaching to remove another old dressing. Ru scooted off immediately to provide a new one.

"Will it be like that in the Impression?" Nian asked. "We will hear a dragon's voice in our heads?"

"Yes, that's how it happens," and C'tic had the same soft expression on his face as H'ran had had.

"And you can always hear them?" Nian asked. "I can usually hear my twin brother—especially if he's in trouble."

"Ah, I thought you two looked alike."

"Oh, we're not completely alike," Nian said. "Neru's much smarter and stronger. He'll make a splendid dragonrider."

"You both will," C'tic surprised her by saying.

"How do you know that?"

"My dragon told me so," C'tic said, and his smile was kind, not teasing.

Two more dressings were needed and then C'tic thanked them for their assistance.

"Can we help again?" Nian asked.

That will depend on what happens at the Hatching, Brith replied himself. *But I would be glad of such light fingers. Maybe you should train to be a dragon healer.*

Nian blinked, startled by his remark.

"Well, you could, you know," Ru said, regarding his sister with some pride. "You're always tending the injured at the Hold."

"Come along, now, candidates," H'ran said. "It is nearly dinnertime."

"Oh, good," Ru said, rubbing his hands together. "I'm hungry."

"Wash your hands well," C'tic said, pointing to a sink to one side of the infirmary. "Remember, you've been handling numbweed. If you don't scrub your hands thoroughly now, some of the numbweed may rub off on your lips when you start eating. Believe me, I know, it's no fun trying to eat your food when your lips are completely numb. Added to that, you'll slobber all over yourself and not even realize it. Not a pretty sight!" While their laughter subsided, the candidates used the scrubbing brushes at the sink and lathered their hands with sweetsand until their skin was rubbed red. As they washed, aromatic odors wafted in their direction and promised a fine meal. By the time they reached the Lower Cavern, weyrfolk were setting generous platters and bowls on the table for them to serve themselves.

"Hey, this is great food," Neru said after he took his first heaping forkful.

"It's meat, you mean," Nian said, teasing her brother.

"Makes a great change from all that fish," Neru replied, selecting yet another slice from the platter in the center of the table.

"Just don't make a pig of yourself here," she added in a low tone so no one else would hear her. "We've never gone hungry, you know, and we must uphold the honor of Lado Hold."

"Humph," Neru grunted and gestured around the table where the other candidates were equally as diligent in reducing the contents of the various serving dishes. "Tell that to the others."

"I wouldn't dream of it," Nian said with great dignity.

After some of the young weyrfolk cleared the table, the Weyrleader at the head table got to his feet.

"As I'm sure you've noticed, we have candidates as our guests. The Hatching may even come tonight," he added, and the candidates gasped as one. He grinned at them. "We are ever at our dragons' pleasure. But all is ready for their arrival. Thank you all for coming at such short notice. If you have any questions, please ask the dragonrider nearest you or our good H'ran. Remember, they were once candidates just like you. And just as nervous!"

"He's nice. Just like our Holder," Nian murmured to her brother.

"But Hatching in the middle of the night?" Ru said. "That's awkward."

She sniffed and then saw a man in harper blue, carrying a gitar, place a stool on the platform and settle himself. He strummed a chord, and people from the audience began shouting for the songs they wanted to hear.

"Oh, I could get used to this," Nian said, settling back. The evenings when Harper Ruart entertained the Hold and everyone was allowed to listen were special to her. Briefly she wondered if the harper played every evening for the Weyr. He struck up some melody she'd never heard before, and

suddenly the air was full of fire lizards. They either went to sit on the shoulders of the people they were beholden to, or found themselves a perch somewhere in the kitchen cavern. They picked up the tune and sang a descant, and the singing was magical. Even Nian was bold enough to join in the choruses, while Ru, once he had listened to the melody all the way through, sang a tenor harmony to it. He had such a nice voice. To Nian's mind, he was as good as any harper student, but he would be best, she added firmly in her heart and mind, as a dragonrider.

Then, when the last note had ended, the harper descended and weyrfolk began to rise and circulate among the tables.

"It's been an exciting day for all you candidates," Kilpie said, coming over to their table. "And there will be more chores in the morning—just to keep you busy, of course, till the eggs are ready to hatch. So we will excuse you to your quarters."

"What if they Hatch tonight?" Robina asked.

"In that case, you'll know about it," Kilpie assured her, giving her what Nian thought was a dismissive look. Nian almost felt sorry for the Masterfarmer's daughter, but Robina did not look at all unsettled.

Actually, Nian was quite willing to have an early night. So much had happened today, and she was tired. She wanted a bath, too, and thought that if she hurried, she'd be able to be first to claim one of the few bathing cubicles in the girls' necessary. She told Neru her wish and he grinned.

"Yeah, I heard there's always hot water here," he said. "I may just have a bath, too. Can't Impress a dragon stinking of fish, you know."

"We do not stink of fish," she said, sniffing at him, although she could catch a tiny whiff of fish oil and sea. "It's marvelous not to have to wait to heat up enough for a decent bath just this once."

So they walked on ahead of the other candidates, grabbing washing things and the towels their mother had packed, to get to a bath before anyone else thought of it.

Nian was lounging in the tub of deliciously hot water by the time other girls thought of bathing. She smiled to herself that she'd been first. She washed her hair, too, in the special shampoo her mother made. "To keep it silky and sweet-smelling," her mother had said. "I can't abide the smell of fish on everything," she invariably added with a long-suffering sigh.

Once, Nian had asked her mother why she had chosen her father, if she didn't like the smell of fish.

"Well, I married him for several reasons. The first is because I love him and he asked me. The second is that he had inherited his father's holding and I didn't know that the place reeked of fish oil and that it's hard to wash scales off a plank floor. But he's a good man, your father, and we've never gone hungry even if it was only fish for supper." Then her mother added plaintively, "I do fancy a taste of beef now and then, and he's willing to spend good credits to see I have some."

Someone rattling the bath door startled Nian out of her memories.

"You were the first in," she heard Robina's sour voice accusing her. "When *are* you going to finish?"

"When I'm clean enough," Nian replied firmly.

"Oh, the twinling from the fish hold. I suppose it's as well if we let you get really clean."

Robina's nasty comment irritated Nian no end. She was really tired of being teased. "I'll hurry, since I know you'd like to get all the sand out of your hair," she said in her sweetest tone of voice, recalling the sight of the unconscious Robina on the sandy floor of the infirmary.

"I'll thank you not to refer to that," Robina said angrily.

"Oh, dear me, I didn't meant to upset you," Nian said without a trace of apology.

"Just give others a turn at a bath!"

"Oh, stop nagging, Master's daughter," someone else called, and Nian could hear Robina stamping away from her door.

"Who said that?" she demanded.

"Another fisherman's daughter," and Nian smiled because she recognized the voice as Orla's.

However, she was clean enough, her hair sufficiently rinsed, so she pulled the plug. As the water audibly swirled out of her tub, she dried herself slowly, then used the towel to wrap her hair up on her head. It would take time to dry, but it really wasn't fair for her to monopolize a bathing cubicle. As she exited, she saw there were six or seven girls waiting. Robina was pacing down at the far end of the facility, so Nian gestured for the nearest girl to quickly claim the bathing cubicle.

"What the—I was next!" she heard Robina yell as she left the necessary.

"You were down at the other end of the room," one of the girls replied ingenuously.

"I should have been next," Nian heard Robina complain, and then Nian was too far away to hear what answer the farmer's daughter got to that protest.

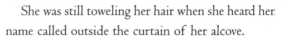

She was still toweling her hair when she heard her name called outside the curtain of her alcove.

"May I come in, Nian?" asked Orla.

"Yes, certainly," she said and her friend slipped in. Orla's curls were still damp from her bath and her face was shiny from washing. "That Robina's something, isn't she?"

"Did someone finally give her a chance to bathe?"

Orla rolled her brown eyes. "Finally. I think her remark about fish smells made her enormously unpopular. How did she get to be so arrogant? I've never met another Master's daughter like her."

"She's very pretty," Nian said wistfully.

"And she thinks that she's going to Impress a queen dragon. Huh!" Orla commented.

"I doubt that," Nian said bluntly. "You heard what R'dik said about not guaranteeing anything. And being squeamish enough to faint while dressing those wounds surely must act against her."

"It was Robina who fainted? I couldn't quite see from where I was in the infirmary. But I'll say frankly enough that the wounds I saw were stomach-churning."

"Brith's, too." Nian shuddered.

"But *you* didn't faint, did you? Nor did I," Orla said. "It'll be interesting to see whom the queen does choose. Can I help you dry your hair, Nian? I'd give anything for straight hair."

"If you had it, you wouldn't want it. But yes, I'd appreciate the help immensely," Nian replied and, finding the second towel in her sack, handed it to her friend. She was tired and her arms ached from rubbing her thick, heavy hair.

The next morning Nian heard a pleasant gong being struck enthusiastically and had a time trying to remember where she was. Lado Hold had a siren that went off each morning, or in stormy times, to assemble people to help in emergencies. She hoped that her chore that morning would involve helping Brith and C'tic. She wanted to ask if it was possible for a candidate to be preselected. She didn't care which kind of dragon she Impressed, or even if she Impressed at all, just as long as Neru succeeded. She'd be grateful no matter what color dragon fancied her brother as his rider. But she saw him as a bronze rider, leading his own wing at Threadfall as he had always daydreamed.

When the candidates were seated and bowls of porridge were being passed to them, H'ran came around with a list, checking names off as he told each person what chore they would have that morning. Nian had a chance to look around the half-filled dining area, wondering where the others were, for last night the cavern had been full.

"Nian?" H'ran had reached her and she smiled up at him. "C'tic asked for you and your brother to assist him with Brith. You have such deft hands."

"Thank you, H'ran," she said, turning with a happy grin to her brother.

Neru went back to spooning porridge into his mouth, seemingly not upset that his sister was the object of special attention. "Good porridge."

"Yes, it is." Nian looked fondly at the brother who hadn't an ounce of jealousy in him.

The candidates were all offered second helpings of the porridge and then served toasted bread with redberry jam.

"So we're both on infirmary duty," Neru said. "We do work well as a team, Ni." Then he cocked his head to one side as if he were trying to hear something barely audible. Nian gave him a querying look, which he simply shrugged off.

Then Nian caught what must have alerted him—a definite humming noise, soft but growing louder. She shifted on her chair, planting her feet firmly on the ground, and felt the sound reverberate through the soles of her feet to the top of her head. It was a lovely sound, reassuring, loving, full of eager anticipation: an anticipation that began to vibrate in her body in time with its immediacy. She cocked her head at her brother and he grinned. As one they rose to their feet just as H'ran approached their table.

"I can see that some of you have already heard the dragons humming. It is time!" he exclaimed. "Their timing is good," he added, a broad smile on his face as he turned toward the candidates' table. "We've all been able to finish our breakfast. All right, candidates please go to your alcoves and change into your white robes. Then come to the Hatching Ground as quickly as possible. You may move among the eggs, if you wish, or just stand still, waiting to see which egg holds the hatchling that wants you as its rider. This is a big moment in the Weyr's life and a bigger one in yours. Go, change. Now!" And with a loud clap of his hands, he dismissed them from the dining hall.

Nian had to wait for Ru to change. He must still be wondering if he should proceed with the deception. He also spent time fussing with his robe, using his own old leather to belt it. Nian did not tell him that that made the robe look even more like a dress.

She'd rushed off to the necessary as anxiety made her feel the need. The trip gave her time to wash her face and hands, too, slightly sticky from the redberry jam. Her stomach was roiling with apprehension, too full of all the food she had consumed to be comfortable. Robina was also in the washroom, vigorously brushing her blond hair with her fingers.

"I don't think the dragons will notice your hair, Robina," Nian said encouragingly, but the girl glared at her.

"That's all *you* know, twinling," she snapped back, a petulant expression on her face. Her brushing increased in vigor, and she swore when she saw that sand still fell from her locks. "Let me alone," she added nastily.

Nian was quite willing to and went to join her twin. Then, side by side, Nian and Neru rushed across the Bowl to the Hatching Ground. The sight of the eggs lying on the hot sands stopped them in their tracks at the arch and then, as they entered, the hot sands made them shift their feet in discomfort. Nian got her first sight of the two dragon parents, standing to the back of the Hatching Ground, watching the candidates making their way among the scattered eggs. The golden queen was huge, and her bronze mate was not much smaller. Nian eased herself behind her brother's sturdy figure, suddenly awed by the sight of such immense dragons.

Nian glanced anxiously at the egg she had liked and was relieved that no one else was near it. Maybe Robina would be too disturbed about her sanded hair to hover nearby. No one was near the egg Ru had singled out. Together they walked across the sands and saw that the other candidates, in their white robes, had spread out on the Hatching Ground. Nian still wondered how the dragons would know which person they should Impress—the Hatching Ground was so big, and the candidates were numerous. She looked around for Orla and Chaum and saw them standing to her right. Around the Hatching Ground, the spectator area was filling up with those invited to share this magical moment. Nian was disappointed that her mother and father weren't among those seated in the gallery; she knew they'd have attended if they could. But at least she had gotten Neru onto the Hatching Ground. Now a hatchling simply must see what a splendid rider Neru would be!

Nian's boots were heating up and she hoped it wouldn't be long before the eggs actually started to hatch. Definitely, she should not have filled up on breakfast. Her stomach felt sour with her building anxiety. She would die of shame if she spewed up all that porridge and redberry jam. She moved closer to Ru, hoping that no one was staring at her.

The hum of the dragons was intensifying. "Look!" Neru said, pointing to the nearest egg. It was rocking in its little depression of sand.

A stir in the gallery suggested that others had seen the movement. There was also a cracking sound that echoed in the vaulted Hatching Ground, and the queen swung her head to stare at the egg. It wasn't far from Neru and Nian, and they could see the crack splitting the eggshell. They held their breaths as the crack girdled the egg and something—a wingtip, Nian thought—protruded from the shell. It split neatly in half and its occupant began to emerge. When the glistening little bronze finally exited its shell, she wondered that it had been able to cram so much body into such a small space.

"A bronze first is a good sign," she heard H'ran murmur as applause came from the gallery.

The queen spread her wings and, lifting herself high on her powerful hindquarters, bugled a welcome to the little bronze. Several other eggs were either rocking or cracking, and Nian didn't know where to look first.

"Nian!" Her brother's startled cry swung her gaze back to him and he pointed to her favorite among the eggs. It was splitting along its axis, and suddenly the top half splintered into shards that were scattered all over as a moist golden head emerged. Robina was already hastening toward the little queen, though she was clutching at her stomach as she approached. It amused Nian that the snotty Robina was also subject to nausea and nervousness.

"Go after the bronze, Ru," Nian said, pushing him toward the wandering hatchling.

"He knows where he's going," Ru said, pointing, and it became obvious to Nian that the hatchling was heading as straight as an arrow toward a tall boy who had sat next to Ru at breakfast.

Greens and blues were now making their choices among the candidates, and weyrfolk were handing out bowls of food, instructing the newly Impressed on how to feed the starving hatchlings.

I'm hungry! Very hungry, a voice said clearly in Nian's head. But she paid no attention to that, since all the hatchlings around her were being fed. There were several eggs toward the back of the Hatching Ground that were rocking and splitting. She tugged on the sleeve of her brother's tunic.

"Let's go over there. No one else is nearby."

He tried to struggle free. "If one of them wants me, it can find me."

"You have got to Impress, Ru," she said, reestablishing her hold on him and hauling him to where he stood the best chance of doing so.

"Maybe the hatchlings know I shouldn't be here as a candidate," was his gloomy reply.

"Nonsense!"

Suddenly, she tripped, or rather was tripped, and sprawled facedown in the hot sands, as something quite heavy seemed to be scratching its way up her exposed back.

What's the matter with you? Can't you hear me? the same voice said petulantly. *I'm hungry. I need to be fed. Are you listening in there?* Something hard tapped on her head.

"Nian, it's the queen. That's the queen on your back, Ni, the queen!" she heard Neru exclaim excitedly.

"But it's you who must Impress, Neru," she said querulously. Oh, her family would never forgive her. Ru would never forgive her.

I will forgive you, if you'll feed me, Nian, the voice said. *My name is Quinth. Why are you avoiding me? I love you. You are mine.*

"Here, help me, H'ran," the Weyrwoman said. "The poor child won't able to get up. Quinth, now get off your rider before you flatten her."

Nian felt the weight being lifted off her, but her

nose had started to bleed and she had to spit blood out of her mouth and shake sand out of her hair. Hands under her armpits assisted her to her feet and then a bowl was thrust into her hands and she looked around and saw golden Quinth, struggling to be free of the hands that held her from going to her chosen rider.

Nian felt two distinct emotions—immense surprise and total dismay.

You don't like me? the dragon asked, her head drooping with disappointment and her wings sagging to the sand.

It's not a question of liking you, Quinth, Nian replied, reaching out her free hand to run her fingers down the little dragon's head to the chin, which she then lifted up. The dragon's eyes, golden with love, met hers and a shiver of absolute delight went down Nian's back. *It's just that I shouldn't Impress unless my brother does, too.*

While we wait for that to happen, the little queen said imperiously, *you may feed me, Nian. I'm starving.*

Remembering the bowl in her hand, Nian grabbed a handful of the meat cubes and offered them to Quinth, who bolted them down so quickly that Nian could see the outline of the mass slide down her neck. Then Quinth opened her mouth again, and again, and again. Nian was forced to sniff in the blood that was oozing from her nose and blot the stream on her sleeve, leaving a red smear behind it.

"Someone bring a cold towel and some numbweed," the Weyrwoman was calling. "Nian, Quinth's rider, has a bloody nose. How very awkward, my dear." The Weyrwoman offered Nian her clean handkerchief. "They don't really mean to hurt anyone in an Impression," she said, "but it was obvious Quinth wanted you and you simply didn't realize that she was headed toward you the moment her shell cracked." She gave a little laugh. "Queens are very determined." That seemed to be a good trait, judging by the indulgence in the Weyrwoman's voice.

"How did it happen that *she* was chosen by the queen and not me?" demanded Robina, standing in front of them, pointing an accusatory finger at Nian

I didn't choose her, Quinth said to Nian, flicking a wingtip at Robina in dismissal.

"Well, this is outrageous!" Robina retorted, as she dodged Quinth's wing tip for fear of being pushed onto the hot sands. When she regained her balance, Robina placed her hands on her hips while tapping one toe in the sands.

"There are green dragons hatching, Robina," the Weyrwoman said pleasantly, pointing to the right. As Nian glanced in that direction, she saw Orla patting a green dragon with one hand and shoving meat toward it with the other.

"They are the most valuable dragons in Threadfall," the Weyrwoman said. "And far more difficult to train. Take a challenge once in your lifetime, Robina. It would do you good."

Eyes wide with outrage, Robina stamped toward the exit, head high. Amazingly enough, a shiny wet green dragonet was stumbling after her as fast as it could make its legs go.

"Oh, no! Almost all the hatchlings have Impressed. Neru *must* be a dragonrider—it shouldn't have been me!" Nian protested in an undertone. Looking around for her twin, she found him standing back by his favorite egg. She could see the thin line of a crack on the side bulge of the egg and Neru was crouched beside it, hands balled in fists as he verbally encouraged its occupant.

"Come on now, that last crack was a good one. Another one and you'll be out."

Nian stuffed another handful of meat into Quinth's mouth and then headed toward her brother. The Weyrwoman held her back, shaking her head. "We have discovered that if an egg doesn't crack on its own, the occupant is probably damaged and it is best to leave nature to take her course."

"And let the dragon die?" Nian was appalled.

A weyrperson approached them proffering damp towels, one of which the Weyrwoman pressed to the nape of Nian's neck. Nian gasped at the cold feel of it. With her other hand, the Weyrwoman used the other cloth to mop the blood off Nian's face and smeared some numbweed on the bridge of her nose. Embarrassed at being tended by the Weyrwoman herself, Nian gently took the cloth and finished mopping her nose and face. And someone else handed her a second bowl of meat.

I am still hungry, Nian, if you don't mind, Quinth told her in no uncertain tones, crossing in front of her. *I am sorry I made your nose bleed.*

A wave of love washed over Nian and she turned adoring eyes on her new lifelong partner. *Oh, sorry my love, I forgot!* And she shoved a larger than usual handful at her queen.

Quinth butted Nian, a nudge that would have been strong enough to make the girl lose her balance if Quinth had not immediately stepped in front of her to prevent her from falling.

A Hatchling must break his own shell? she asked her dragon.

It shows the strength of the dragon within, Quinth informed her.

How do you know that? You're only just hatched yourself.

There are things dragons know instinctively about other dragons, Quinth replied with a faint reproof in her mental tone.

But my brother has *to Impress,* Nian said in almost a moan, her eyes on the shell of the egg beside her brother, who was stroking the casing and urging its occupant to try again.

It is as hungry as I was, Quinth told Nian. *It only needs food.*

Tell the Weyrwoman so we can break its shell for Neru.

There are some things one must do for one's self, Quinth replied. *I made it and I was hungry. I am still hungry.*

As Nian scraped another handful of meat out of the bowl, nearly the last, she had a sudden, decisive idea.

"Well, I'll need more food for you then, you splendid bottomless pit," she said aloud and saw that their way to the entrance of the Hatching Ground lay past Neru and the cracked but as yet unbroken shell. "Let's go that way," and she nudged Quinth slightly to one side so they would pass right by the egg in a few steps. As they drew closer, Nian turned to her dragon with beseeching eyes.

Now, Quinth dear queen, can you trip me up again as we pass by?

Trip you up? Why should I do that? You bleed!

Just trip me, Nian repeated, slowing her steps so that she would not pass by her objective.

What a strange thing you ask me to do, Quinth replied.

You had no trouble doing it before. Do it now!

Quinth did so with such energy and precision that Nian fell right across the top of the egg, the heavy bowl in her hands smashing through the eggshell. Immediately a moist bronze head pushed through the opening and, as the hatchling also pushed its shoulders against the front of the shell, he was able to make his way out and onto the sands, peering around him. Then as Neru held his hand out to touch the hatchling's head, the creature looked up, its multi-faceted eyes whirling orange with excitement and its tongue came out and licked Neru's hand.

Like a blaze in her head, Nian felt the force of a new personality come between her and the long-term bond with her brother. It was almost as if that bond was being erased and she cried out as she clung weakly to Quinth. But Neru's Impression to the little bronze had been completed.

"My dragon's name is Larinth!" Neru shouted loudly for all to hear as tears of joy ran down his cheeks.

I'm starving! I'm starving, the little dragon said piteously, butting at Neru to succor him.

Do not worry, my brave dragon, I will feed you until you're stuffed full, Neru said as he stroked the ridges above his dragon's eyes.

"Neru, grab some of this meat and feed your dragon," Nian said, struggling to help her brother and grateful that there was still some meat in her bowl.

Quinth roared with anger that her own rider would feed her food to another's dragon. But three riders instantly leaped to help and Nian stuffed Quinth until her mouth was so full that the little queen had to start chewing or choke. Neru was given a full bowl and Nian's was replaced so that very shortly both the gold and the little bronze were contented.

H'ran and the Weyrwoman began examining the bronze dragon, opening and closing its wet wing membranes, tapping its chest, checking its legs and tail to be sure it was healthy.

"He keeps saying that he was so weak with hunger, it was hard to make the shell crack, but see, he had almost broken through when Nian tripped,"

Neru was saying, stroking his dragon. "He's wonderful, isn't he?"

"He certainly seems whole and healthy," was H'ran's decision, although he looked to the Weyrwoman to see if she agreed.

Oh, he is, he is, Quinth said to Nian.

"So, was your stumble accidental?" the Weyrwoman asked, looking from Nian to Quinth. "After what I had just told you?"

"She was trying to get the last of the meat in the bowl," Nian said, boldly staring back at the Weyrwoman.

I am still hungry, Quinth said as if that justified everything. Dutifully, Nian held out another handful, careful to see that every piece went into the queen's mouth. *It was sheer luck that I had enough strength to break my own shell,* Quinth added, swallowing the last mouthful before she pointed her head at Nian. *And then you kept walking away from me!*

I am sorry, dearling, Nian said as contritely as she could, holding out another handful of meat. *I simply never thought that I'd Impress a dragon.*

"Well, we're all here now, and together," Nian said, "and Larinth looks like a fine fellow."

Thank you, Larinth said, his eyes glowing as he regarded Nian and Quinth intently.

Beside her, Quinth said quite distinctly, *You're welcome*. Obviously, she didn't like Nian to have much to do with Larinth. But then that's what H'ran had said about newly Impressed dragons. They were jealous of their new partners.

"Let us help you toward the barracks then, Nian and Neru, and settle your dragons," the Weyrwoman suggested.

"No more staggering into me either, please, Quinth," Nian said, passing her the last of the food in this latest bowl. "Can she have more?" she queried the Weyrwoman dubiously.

"She'll probably need it," the Weyrwoman said. "After all, it's a long walk for a newly hatched dragonet."

Somehow, Nian did not think she had fooled the Weyrwoman with her desperate ploy but Neru *had* Impressed a bronze and that was justification enough. Sometimes things just needed a little push to come right.

One small detail, Quinth said in a firm mental tone, *I am your dragon. And Larinth is your brother's. Let us keep that in order.*

Of course, dear Quinth, of course. I am all yours.

Yes, you are, and Quinth moved as close to Nian as she could.

"Hey, watch it, Quinth, you can't sit on my lap, you know," Nian spoke out loud to her dragon. "I've already got a bloody nose and sore ribs from you knocking me about. Can we please make it back to our weyr in an orderly fashion?" And a gentle note crept into Nian's voice that took the sting out of her words.

Of course, Quinth replied in a suspiciously demure tone. As they passed H'ran, he put yet another bowl of meat cubes into Nian's hand and gave her the barest smile and a wink that Nian decided to ignore. After all, her plan had worked.

Just then, Conna came forward to congratulate Nian. She saw Neru with Larinth and raised her shoulders in a shrug. Nian held her breath. Would Conna tell the Weyrwoman that her twin's candidacy was dubious? At last Conna's eyes met hers. The green rider merely grinned.

"It is always what the hatchling decides, my dear," she said kindly. "And I'm very pleased for all your sakes."

Nian leaned weakly against her queen for support. And Quinth graciously supported her. She kept a hand on her dragon's neck as they proceeded on their way to the weyrling barracks.

Halfway across the Hatching Ground, they saw Robina patiently feeding the little green dragon that had pursued her half across the Bowl to succeed in making Impression. Robina's expression was that of a love-struck young woman, and her little green dragon looked ecstatic.

"Well," H'ran said, "I think those two are well suited. And our little queen has done the best for herself. Now I must busy myself to ensure that all my new weyrlings are securely settled in their weyrs; they'll need to sleep. Follow me as you will, young dragonriders. Or should I say follow me, Nian, rider of golden Quinth and, N'ru, rider of bronze Larinth?" H'ran's kindly tone was not lost on the twins and they smiled in unison at the man who would teach them all they'd need to know about dragons. Neru stood all the taller when he heard the Weyrlingmaster use his newly contracted name, the sign to all on Pern that he was, indeed, a dragonrider.

As Nian and Neru walked together off the hot sands and toward the weyrs, each closely escorting their dragons, they saw the crowd who had witnessed their Impressions slowly take their leave of the gallery around Ista Weyr's Hatching Ground. Life was returning to normal for those spectators, but it had just begun for Nian and Neru. A pensive air settled over the twins as they encouraged their dragons onward to the weyrling barracks.

Both Quinth and Larinth were exhausted as their riders gently steered them toward the nearest unoccupied beds. Quinth settled herself in, and as soon as her head lay on her forelegs, she fell immediately and deeply asleep.

With a deep, satisfied sigh, Nian clambered up next to her golden dragon, and rested her head on Quinth's right foreleg, curling her body up close to her dragon's. Nian inhaled the dragon's scent; spicy, like the kitchen at Lado before a big Gather. Spicy and slightly meaty, as the little queen breathed down on her rider. And comforting as if they had known each other forever, just as Nian and Neru had known each other all their lives.

"Ni?" Nian heard Ru's voice gently calling to her from her left. "Larinth is fast asleep and I just wanted to . . ." Ru's voice faltered and Nian immediately rose from her perch and found her brother in the passageway. Most of the other new riders were already asleep and several were snoring.

"What is it, Ru?" Nian asked, concern coloring her voice.

"I . . . I just wanted to tell you. Oh, Shards! Thanks Ni, for everything you—"

"Hush," Nian interrupted her brother. "You don't ever have to thank me. You are my twin."

"But I want to, Ni." And he raked a hand through his thick hair before continuing. "Back at Lado, when the dragons came on Search, I was so gobsmacked that the dragons didn't select me right away, I couldn't do or say anything. I . . ." It was obvious to Nian that her younger brother was struggling to say something of great importance to him. She reached out and clasped his hand tightly, he responded but then gently shook his hand free of her grip. Straightening his shoulders, Neru stood resolutely and looked his sister squarely in the eyes.

"I've never felt this before, Ni, but back at Lado I was jealous that the dragons Searched you first and only took me along as an afterthought. I'm sorry, Ni, I've never been jealous of you before in all my life. But when I thought you were going to Impress a dragon and I wouldn't, I—I felt gutted." He lowered his head then, mumbling, "I thought you were stealing my dream."

Nian took a step closer to her brother and gently

tilted his chin upward until his eyes were forced to meet hers.

"But, Ru," Nian exclaimed, "I felt the same way too! I was afraid that I'd steal your dream and leave you—all in the same day! I didn't want our separation to be that way." They looked at each other in silence for a time, and then Ru spoke gently to his twin.

"You know, Ni, even though we both have dragons, the moment we Impressed our separation began."

"But what do you mean? We're both here in the same weyr," Nian said, suddenly remembering the strange jolt of emotion she felt when Neru Impressed Larinth.

"You are a queen rider now, Nian, and I a bronze. You and Quinth may be sent to another Weyr, and I will remain here at Ista. And, as a queen rider, your duties will be far different from mine." He gave a little laugh and then grinned warmly at his sister. "Being dragonriders has more effectively separated us than if we'd been sent to opposite ends of Pern. It's ironic, isn't it?"

From Quinth's sleeping ledge, and beyond, where Larinth slept, the twins heard their dragons rumbling. Two large dragon eyes opened, whirling in blue, and peered at them from the darkness of Quinth's bed.

Separate you may be, but Larinth and I, your dragons, will always keep you together. You'll never be more than a thought apart—and you'll never be alone, golden Quinth assured the twin dragonriders.